A DIRGE
FOR THE WILL TO LIVE

A DISJOINTED SEARCH FOR THE WILL TO LIVE

SHAKA N'ZINGA

FOREWORD BY ROBIN D.G. KELLEY
AFTERWORD BY MARC SALOTTE
A WORD FOR AN ELDER BY IDRIS ALAOMA

**SOFT SKULL PRESS
BROOKLYN, NY**

A DIJOINTED SEARCH FOR THE WILL TO LIVE
ISBN: 1-887128-77-8
COPYRIGHT ©2003 SHAKA N'ZINGA

FIRST EDITION
FEBRUARY 2003

EDITORIAL: CHRISTOPHER TERET & MARC SALOTTE
DESIGN: DAVID JANIK
LANDSCAPE PHOTOGRAPHY: KIMBERLY ROGERS

PRINTED IN CANADA

DISTRIBUTED BY PUBLISHERS GROUP WEST
WWW.PGW.COM | 800.788.3123

PUBLISHED IN COORDINATION WITH
SEXPOL EDITIONS/CLAUSTROPHOBIA COLLECTIVE
WWW.CHARM.NET/~CLAUSTRO/

SOFT SKULL PRESS
71 BOND STREET
BROOKLYN, NY 11217

WWW.SOFTSKULL.COM

CONTENTS

FOREWORD BY ROBIN D. G. KELLEY   V

A DISJOINTED SEARCH FOR THE WILL TO LIVE   1

AFTERWORD BY MARC SALOTTE   139

A WORD FROM AN ELDER BY IDRIS ALAOMA   147

FOREWORD | ROBIN D. G. KELLEY

A Disjointed Search for the Will to Live is neither memoir nor novel, poetry nor history. It is all these things and more, much more. It is a plunge into the depths of the unconscious, a meditation on freedom, a New Afrikan Manifesto for liberation, a commentary on terrorism and the criminal justice system, a withering attack on the black bourgeoisie around the globe, an appeal for environmental justice, a prayer for the purification of the land, a powerful indictment of capitalism, a critique of the prison house we call Western Civilization . . . and a love story.

From the very outset of this book, we learn what drives Mr. N'Zinga's will to live: a dream of freedom and a will to struggle, not merely for his own survival but for the transformation of community, the liberation of humanity. Finding his will to live also means accepting a willingness to die for freedom. He recognized at a very young age what Malcolm X also recognized at a very young age: that he had to re-make himself before he could struggle to re-make the world. Becoming a revolutionary, a "New Afrikan man" as he puts it, requires education, reflection, knowledge of history and self, a deep sense of empathy for oppressed people but a refusal to accept victim-status. "The 'Will to Freedom,'" he writes, "has to be present in the person, the people, the clan, the nation, if such a new creation of self, by self, is to be carried off." Throughout this book, Mr. N'Zinga proclaims the humanity of the millions of kidnapped Afrikans and their descendants, not only be recounting their suffering but exposing their vulnerabilities, their violence toward each other, their mistakes and confusions, the wholeness of their lives and loves.

Love. It's all through this book, the heart of Mr. N'Zinga's revolutionary vision. Indeed, he made me think of that 19th century English romantic socialist William Morris who struggled to build a new society rooted in "the ethic of cooperation, the energies of love." For Mr. N'Zinga, the realm of love is expansive, extending from romantic love and love of community to love of self. Just about everyone, except thy enemy. He doesn't go that far, in part because lust in the guise of love is used here as a metaphor to understand black people's seduction. The white she-devil is the United States, she's capitalism and imperialism, she's the destructive consumer culture that has promoted violence among ourselves over commodities that are supposed to make us feel cool and special and powerful. Mr. N'Zinga is saying, on the one hand, we better watch out for those who claim they "love us," those who can ignite our (false?) desires, those before whom we lose control. On the other hand, he is calling us on a true quest for love, a new communion with the many who share our history and have been consumed by its tragic dimensions; a true romantic love based on care, respect, honesty, intimacy, partnership, and a united "will to freedom" in all realms of life; a true self-love, without which we are unable to love others. It is a remarkable insight from someone who has spent half of his life locked down in a facility run on the energies of hate.

Like Malcolm, Assata Shakur, George Jackson, Angela Davis, Mumia Abu-Jamal, and Antonio Gramsci, Mr. N'Zinga is not just a cause célèbre, a victim of the system, but one of our theorists, a deep thinker and critic whose reflections about fascism under fascism offer fruitful insights for the coming struggles. And like all of these imprisoned intellectuals, his primary concern is not the condition of prisons. On the contrary, throughout the book it is clear that even his prison stories extend far beyond the Maryland state correctional facility that currently cages him. His analysis reaches beyond the United States. He takes on the world and expresses both the tragic dimensions of our history under racial capitalism and imperialism as well as possibility under revolution. And his analysis is unflinching, taking on Marxism and Anarchism for their limitations and calling on all of us to generate new ideas, new insights. Several times Mr. N'Zinga suggests that we emancipate ourselves from texts that were products of earlier revolutionary movements. Echoing the radical theorist Cedric Robinson, Mr. N'Zinga reminds us that for all of Marxism's emancipatory potential, it was tainted with the same European culturalist assumptions that informed white supremacy and the imperial order. He writes, "From Hegel to Lenin the dialectics, the revolutions, the international communist this and that was in reality the same thing Locke and all the other capitalist parasitic thinkers were proposing: the domination of european culture, thought, and practices; white supremacy and nationalism."

Now them is fightin' words! But before you Marxist revolutionaries of varying ideological stripes get too defensive, I urge you to pay attention to what Mr. N'Zinga is trying to say here. Just as old Karl himself said "I'm not a Marxist," Mr. N'Zinga is calling for us to open our imaginations, recognize that Marxism is a product of its own time and place and was never meant to be a dogma. He doesn't reject dialectical thinking so much as the way dialectics has been employed. Mr. N'Zinga demands that we begin with human reality, with pain and suffering, with actual lived experience. "What is required today is a new way of thinking, seeing, and acting upon the world, in unison with the world as it acts upon us in return. The dialectical materialism of Marx, the leftist, the anarchist, and the other so-called deep thinkers that deal with 'thesis, antithesis, and synthesis,' negate much of the reality, and all the spirit of humanity—they have no idea of the human face of the thesis, the base nature of the antithesis, thus their synthesis always falls short of creating that which is supposed to negate the ugly reality of capitalist man's insane world order."

Marxism and other socialist visions have not effectively struggled with capitalism's psychological assault on our humanity, which at its heart includes the problem of racism, nationalism, patriarchy, the destruction of the environment, and sexual oppression. While Marx and his writing partner, Frederich Engels, were well familiar with conquest, genocide, slavery and slavery's demise, their materialist conception of history lacked the tools to understand the psychological dimensions of exploitation and domination. For that we turn to the likes of Frantz Fanon, or perhaps Aime Cesaire, who not only wrote eloquently of how colonialism "decivilizes" the *colonizer*, propelling all of Europe along the road toward "savagery," but questions the very concept of progress and modernity. For Cesaire, the consequences are not just material but psychic:

> I hear the storm. They talk to me about progress, about 'achievements,' diseases cured, improved standards of living.
>
> I am talking about societies drained of their essence, cultures trampled underfoot, institutions undermined, lands confiscated, religions smashed, magnificent artistic creations destroyed, extraordinary possibilities wiped out.[1]

Mr. N'Zinga reminds me of Cesaire, for his source of knowledge is not in the statistics, the empirical tools often used against us to dehumanize us, but in the poetics of feeling, experience and imagination. Mr. N'Zinga takes us on a wild journey, often traversing hundreds of years, adopting the personas of historical figures at the dawn of the European invasion or projecting forward into a liberatory future. It is easy to document the sorry state of affairs; it's not so easy to capture the pain, sadness and confusion that comes with it. It's easy to identify the sources of exploitation and oppression; it's not so easy to see a way out, to imagine what for too many of us seems impossible—the creation of a completely new society and new people not structured by the capitalist culture into which we were born. How is Mr. N'Zinga able to sustain such a vision in the midst of such intense anger and pain? The answer, I believe, rests in his ability to see beauty in the midst of war. The line that stopped me cold in my tracks was this:

> There is a window in the building, inside the prison, the separates me from the living and acts as a beautiful vista into the life, the world, of which I am denied. Through this window I have a view of the carefree movements and activity of that day unfold before my longing

eyes—done through the window of the prison that holds me; watching a honeybee alight upon a dandelion full of her needed honeymaking sustenance. A wonderful interaction between a wild cat and her litter of six kittens progressive before my eyes, unhindered by the foulness of this blighted concentration camp that now inhibits my ability to be one in free and natural activity with them . . . .

For me, this is one of the most revolutionary passages in *A Disjointed Search*, for it is about seeing the world as possibility, finding in beauty and love the basis for a new civilization based on recognizing life, nature, and communion as fundamental to human desire. The "Tru Braveheart" isn't just a warrior out to destroy all vestiges of the old order but to create new relationships without fear, develop new ways of seeing and feeling based on "the ethic of cooperation, the energies of love." Mr. N'Zinga may disagree with me, but I believe his vision is closer to Dr. Martin Luther King's than he realizes.

Mr. N'Zinga has many more books in him and I'm looking forward to reading all of them. Let's hope the next one will be completed outside of that hell hole in which he now resides, and let me urge all of you to support the struggle to free Shaka N'Zinga and all the other prisoners of war within these United States. Given our current political crises, the war in Afghanistan and who knows where else, the corporatization and immiseration of the world, the growing prison population that now includes Arab and South Asian brothers and sisters caught in the "war on terrorism," the bankruptcy of established black leadership, and the brainwashing of our youth to believe that "getting paid" is the purpose of life. We have much work to do, but unless we can see our own possibility and humanity, unless we can imagine a different future and find beauty amidst the ugliness we now endure, we'll all be stuck in prison.

[i] Aime Cesaire, *Discourse on Colonialism* (New York: Monthly Review Press, 1972 [orig. 1955]), 21.

A DISJOINTED SEARCH FOR THE WILL TO LIVE

PART ONE

I

He was once free, but she,
the child of tainted seduction
and unfettered passion, touched
the baseness of his lower self.
Pushing him back into the embrace
of the primal grip of the dreaded
middle ages.

Like the white plague that
dismayed europa, she touched
his heart.
Unless he say grace,
he shall never be free again.

With a body to die for; a superfluity
of la clitoris to be worshipped and kissed,
she was the all and all of each woman
or man's eroticism. Eyes the like of
fallen autumn leaves, with flickers of
sunshine gold and honey brown, grassy green
and flesh blood red. Her hair the
color of hell fire; she possessing the face
of Gabriel's XXX-wife.

A DISJOINTED SEARCH FOR THE WILL TO LIVE

She gave him the evil eye of love and fresh
blood, the look of the she-devil.
Stalking her prey, taking a
hold of his mind and body desires—claiming
his freedom of choice as her own.
Kissing his hooded phallus, slurping his flesh,
as if she was of the cult of
Phallicist. Drawing from it the seed of life,
spitting it into the sink of the XXX movie
theater's john—where they met.

Making him a slave to every
desire and passion she had for
life and death. Having threeway
sex in the middle of a busy
freeway (I95), with the well preserved
corpses of Jimi Hendrix and James Dean,
as he films it all with camcorder,
hot coffee and donuts, in stolen
cop car.

Taking him into the caverns
of hell, in New York City,
the underworld of the forgotten,
where a mad blood orgy took place—
just to soothe her blood lust for
the grotesque unrecorded slaughter
of those without family or friends.

Coming up the escalator, with the
unmistakable scent of fresh blood
and gore all about their person, she
informs him of the coming end
of love deferred—with the look of

infinite sadness tattooed on her
Bill Gates face...yet and still she
smiled the smile of Bill Clinton.
Telling him this is why it is so
important for her to get her
fill now; for once the gods return,
she whispers to him with pain in each word,
there will be no more allowances
for such debauchery and absurdity
of the living wishing to touch and
embrace the dead.

He could only stare off into
the dead eyes of his own reflection,
like a dead man stares off into death
looking for the light behind life,
imploring the gods—praying them
godspeed—in their return to liberate
him from this incarnation of
humanity lost.

She told him that she loved him almost
as much as she did the castration of the
first born of each family that prayed to
the SUNGOD "RA"...touching him on the
underside of his very vainy shaft, she
did the work of the vampire, looking to
seduce him into protecting her from the
consequences of the coming conversions
to be had in 2003.

With the mark of the beast,
MADE IN THE U.S.A.,
engraved on her shapely

A DISJOINTED SEARCH FOR THE WILL TO LIVE

yet freakish backside, she went on mooning and
winking her brown eye at the
world of the living—having
regard only for the demented.

She touched my heart, unless
I say grace, I will never be
free again.

II

Needing to break the hold that
she, the She-Devil, has on his
mind and soul, he moves out to
free himself. Days of milky haze,
dried glaze donuts, and sleeping
bags, are spent in places deemed
unsuitable for human habitation.

Blazing a trail across the seven continents,
he finds himself in the Sudan—lost but yet
found. Staring into the sun of the old world,
he beseeches the SUNGOD "RA", imploring him to
behold his trembling hands of despair and shame.
Hands which are extended Heavenward, towards
the furthest star in the infinite
universe of the outer world of the gods drunk on
vanity.

Gripped by the unnerving feeling of being followed,
he ceases his journey, and comes to reside at some
coastal town, somewhere in Ghana. Looking to discover
the identity of the idea that follows him, he walks

off into the forest of the doomed and unforgotten souls
of those who perished leaping from ships to freedom, thinking
of home, as they were consumed by sharks, fat from many
a black soul who went before; the black souls who sought home
and freedom in the jaws of the Great White Shark.

It was she who had chained his soul to the wanton neglect of himself and his kind. She was determined to continue to hold him in her grips of fresh blood, foiled sex, and freakest discourse of the absurdity of the gods, their saints, and the coming of love actualized. Touched by a bit of rage, he turned and gave chase, not caring or fearing the power of this creature that he still desired so very much. He bared his fangs, extended his claws, leaping through the jungle air, absent of jungle noises or movement, only to land onto the corpse of an Irish lass once possessed of stunning beauty. He reared onto his hind legs, preparing to feed, when the scent of the insanity of this act almost suffocated him.

With great love of nothing ness, the she-devil continued to whisper in his inner ear, his heart and mind, demanding that he make the sacrifice of the dead, to her, for her. He resisted the call of the wild, the call of the white blight. Painted pictures of the living entered his mind. Befogged and blind, his person became erect, his passion for the dead seemed to become even more excited by these images of the living. Confused, he almost cursed the gods: "Why! Why, do you subject me to such torment of the flesh? Why am I expected to resist the temptations of the mind, the lust for money and the dead things it can buy? To the wind I have through my honor and dignity! Why do you still insist on having me suffer the agony that comes along with consciousness? I did not ask for this! I was born and bred to be a slave, betrayed by my own! And you ask me to give up the materialism I know I can obtain—if only I forsake the reality of you gods! I can feel desire pull at my loins…I can have the world, as the she-devil has shown me, if only I give up the gods…But my soul, the spirit of those who went before, will not allow me to do any of this in peace! Why me, 'RA'!

A DISJOINTED SEARCH FOR THE WILL TO LIVE 8

Why don't you let me be?"

The corpse arose, and from her mouth came the promise of the gods—the promise of eternal life in paradise, in the land of milk and honey, Afrikan pride, unity, and life. Back to his senses, he leaves the forest of the forgotten souls to return to his journey of a million and one lives. "As weak and infirm as you are, as cold and desolate the world, you do have the strength to overcome her hold on you, in spite of it all; in spite of the call of the wild, the call of the beast from within. Yet, it is you who must come to the finality of such a possibility—you and no one else. If you lose yourself, then the struggle will continue. If you succeed, then your tomorrows will be free of this 6000 year long struggle between she and thee."

Surrounded, on all sides, by dark faces. Moving through this buzzing crowd, he cringed as he looked into each face and found that looking back at him were the images of his own face. In each child, he saw the child that he once and still was. In each adult's face he saw the man he had yet to become. In Afrika he saw Amerikkka. Trembling from the cold of having to sleep, of having to dream of the past, of the present, and of the future, he shot up the coke made from the coca leaf, and without much resistance, refused to be about the work of the gods. Though he dreaded having to confront the she-devil, his loins, his lower self still called out to her—beseeching her to perform her mouth magic on his person. In silk robes, driving the finest cars, buying the best clothes, wearing gold, having power and fame, were things of the materialistic world that beckoned him to continue to negate his historical duty—his duty to be brave heart and true.

But he had suffered! He had tasted the lash,
the bite of the butt of the pig's 9mm, called
tasteless names, shoved through schools designed
for fools and slaves. Bred to be fed upon by
the parasitic folk, with gray skin, nasty

smelling hair, and an intense hatred for life.
Trained to be other than himself, mentally
and culturally castrated—he hated himself;
he hated his kind.

Coming down off of the coke high, flying like the wind through the streets of no win, he found himself lost in the nether world of nothing to come. Hanging out with Charlie Parker, smoking dope, nodding out to the fine tones of Miles Davis' cool jazz, and swinging to the beat of erotic escapism that characterized those times, these times, and any times to be after these times of niggas turning tricks for the "MAN". Not caring or daring to think of the time line that he now sleeps in, the 1940s, he bowed down for another smell of death. He was a child of the 70s, raised in the 80s, gone insane by the 90s, now nodding out in the 40s. Nowhere to look but back into the time of the past, the last time dark folk had a bit of class, pride, and neverminded to clash with that wicked she-devil's ass. Moving fast through the time of the have-nots who had the riches of honor and respect. Limping through the tiny hole which separated the then from the now, almost forgetting the promise of the gods, taking unconscious steps toward the liberty bell, he sings "Miss American Pie"!

The slave of passion, the infirm man full of body desires, had found his way back to the center of his inner, rising, flame on, sun-core. Coasting down the dawn of times which call for total revolution, preparing himself for the war of all times. Reading a page from Sun Tzu's *Art of War*—the chapter on waging war—as he has thoughts of Comrade George Jackson. Thinking to himself: "For you George; for we, you died, now for you, we live not in vain…learning to live…and fight. This just ain't being done for you, but for all like you who went before." This was his way of attempting to become more inclined to live for that which he knew he should—for the liberation of the forsaken, the downtrodden, the folk that live with dirt behind their ears, and blood between their toes—the sufferers.

A DISJOINTED SEARCH FOR THE WILL TO LIVE

Feeling the turbulence of the coming storm, in his sleep, free from the missing links found in the space between his ears. Determined not to give in to the evil of that lost part of himself, the evil that is created by the tear in the cultural vortex, the loss of identities purpose and cause, is missed and the void thus created has to be filled in by the creation of the new identity—created by the self as it interacts with the environs, the situational and circumstantial pressures that compel him to develop the will to death for freedom. The "Will to Freedom" has to be present in the person, the people, the clan, the nation, if such a new creation of self, by self, is to be carried off. So it appeared to he whose innards were not far from being ripped asunder by the troubled pull between the need to have and the will to be a free and complete spirit, a man of true pride and grace. He lamented yet sustained!

III

Faces
All the faces and voices of the
dark men that surround me, in
this white constructed den of
torment and demise, ignite
in my mind burning memories of
prodigious times long dead and gone,
erased from the here and now—surviving
only in the database of the spirit of
these men who brought the light of
humanity to the beast now their masters.

All the deferred smiles and abrogated
laughs of the
dark faces of the men now walking in
circles around a yard enclosed by
fences with razor sharp teeth and

flesh disfiguring projectiles
stir within me the images of the
ages of their past greatness,
pride, and honor; images of the
time before the ghost from the
wastelands of the north brought
the end—the time before their civil
nation-states were spoiled by this invader.

The sun-kissed faces—the first to be
thus
blessed—
of these dark men, brings
back the scents of the groves,
now buried underneath time, in
the pageless book of history,
of the Sahara, where the people,
great and small, woman and man,
gathered to discuss the business
of the coming harvest...Nubia.

Oh, the memories of what once was
at the times when there was no guns,
no ownership of human lives, no
stainless steel walls, razor wire,
and broken smiles in visiting halls
full of mother's hugs, infant child's
far off stare, and lover's kisses
goodbye.

All set in dark faces confined
in white places.

IV

Coming to terms with the loss of his innocence, our protagonist moves on to the next life, still trying to evade the lush lips of the unholy Mary. Always engaged in some form of struggle within himself, as he kissed and played with the deformed ideas of she who played at being the mother of all civilization—the she who was really a he dressed in the clothes of a justice, without scale, in the guise of being cultured and social. He, our nameless sufferer, will prevail—so he would like to think. Destined to live the life of a rider, living in the inner jungle of torment and persecution, he vows not to die on his knees. He moves through the streets where the tantalizing hordes of hookers roam, in their see-through smiles, cum-stained red lips, and sea-deep parted thighs. Whispering "blow job for five." Not wanting to return home for fear of an ass whipping, he chases the demons of himself off as they attempt to guide him into the arms of one of the hookers with the see-through smiles—which is the mirror to her hopeless soul. "How dare they!" he screams to his better half, "Know not they that the she-devil is on the prowl? Cannot they feel her presence in the see-through smiles of the walking dead?" He continued on in this vain as he approached the doorway of legalized murder. Stopping only when he saw the empty eyes of the court clerk. Death is so peaceful, yet so deadly! Justice is far from being blind...Off to jail you go.

A life so complicated, so complex, that the misshapen of the world, this world, cannot help but be taken note of by the brave heart and true—the unfortunate few of the suffering masses who can see the reality of this existence for the nightmare that it truly is and can only remain for as long as the stupidity and greed of finance capital remains supreme. "Why try?" asks he of himself. "Why move to attempt to be released from the embrace of western man?" "Life in amerikka wasn't all that bad!" is the thought he had as he watched the forced marching of the children of Afrika, now in amerikkka. "In spite of the racism at least we are able to eat grits and laugh at Bill Cosby; watch BET and read Ebony and Jet...Shit, the price of happiness, for me, is submission! So why not submit?" Grounded into the dirt of the world, hated by your own, forsaken by the gods, why even try? For in this dream he is alone! From no quarter can he look for help, as he is dragged through the streets of downtown Baltimore. With a crowd of death wishers on both sides of the street, he is forced to drag the cross of economic growth and human sacrifice on his back, feet shackled, tarred and feathered, castrated, over the burning hate of the smoldering remains of the millions that traveled the very same road before him. Told to sing to the gods of europe, he smiles, daring their death to overlook him! Yet, deep within himself, he still felt himself not to be strong enough!

He thinks to himself as he drives over the broken records of times past: "I cannot front, my soul is still within the hold of she who hails from some desolate place in Northern europe; Mary be her foul name. I, the child of Afrika, smile at that part of me which refuses to let go of the uncircumcised love of she who dares defy to wonderful commands of Nature and the gods of the universe." This thought of castrated love pushes him head long into a classroom of his youth, wherein he was taught the opposite of the truth. The hatred of life, all life, was the basic premise of all thoughts pushed and taught in these places referred to as the "Killing fields of the minds of god's children"—by those who could see the means to the end of miseducation of the children of Afrika..."Stop! No more beer!" he yells to the bartender, named Rex, with breast, in a diaper, with a dildo attached to his nose. And whispers into his bloody Mary, "I am drunk enough off of the toxic waste of this universal dump, full of the shit of western man's unnatural thoughts, concepts, civilization. The planet earth is full of dark faces and death white minds. I have no need for nothing mind altering. Lost in the mix of this drink, exhausted from the struggle with she who whispers in the ears of my heart. I do not want to listen, but I do...When uncircumcised love calls, I listen and blindly follow—not daring to question the absurdity of the moment."

V

Who am I?

She touched my heart with the promise of a better life, the lies of materialism over the spirit—the love of inanimate objects. I tangled with the devil, I went to bed with the devil, I made love to the devil over 700 centuries ago. I forfeited my right to life when I displaced myself, when I replaced my gods for the gods of another. First it was with the greeks, but I rebounded from this folly; however 2900 years later, I succumbed yet again to the gross thoughts and ways of he who subjugates his woman to the status of beast and prefers to have sex with young boys. Where I saw the world as something to be loved and respected, she saw it as something to be controlled and owned. Where I saw the interconnection between all living things, he saw separation. Where I saw human beings, she saw only herself—all others were hers to own and control; for, in her mind, she was superior. Where my gods commanded the unity of all life, her gods commanded crusades, conquest, and capitalism. I gave her civilization and sanity, she gave me pestilence and death; Materialism and Machiavellianism. The blight of humanity proceeded from her breast, as she called for progress, while taming and slaying the lives and ways of the savages with the savage lies of providence and manifest destiny. But she could not have done these things without my help—I, the coward, the child of selfishness and greed. The sort of coward willing to sell the deceptive comforts of a dead idea of god to a fatherless child.

In the name of Islam, in what is to be considered recent history, I allowed her to lead me into the heart of Afrika, long after the death of the prophet. I converted millions at the point of my sword or gun. At one time in my journey on the path of enslaver of my own, they called me Tippu Tip. Though I was the child of Afrika, I called myself arab and hated my so-called savage and infidel people. From Zanzibar I acted as the pawn of arab imperialism—as slave catcher and Islam pusher. For twenty-six thousand dollars I acted as the pawn of european imperial interest, by serving as guide to the forerunner of the european scramble for Afrikan real estate. Morton Stanley was his name, and for Belgians' imperial interest did he dare journey where no pale face had traveled—into the heart of the Congo. For twenty-six thousand dollars, I sold the future of my own kind to a people he viewed as being little more than nigger with a bit of pig sense. I, the coward, who thought himself arab but in truth was the child of Afrika and the Amerikas is the memory of me, the coward, and they all know in their marrow that if not for me, the world would be free.

Continually, I have allowed myself to be used by the evil that she gives life to; the evil of death in the disguise of brotherly love, humanity, and universality. The veil of brotherly love was presented as the religious ideals of christianity and islam, but when stripped away all one would find was one form of subjugation or another. The guise of humanity was the lie to convince the dark world that the pale world was not out to enslave and feed on them. The nationalism of europe and the arab was given the dress of universality to cover the demented hate that motivated and drove the ambition of these inhuman few. Yet and still, none of this would have been possible if I did not exist…How am I to correct these grave betrayals I have committed throughout the ages of my existence (I, the cowardly man, in the mask of rationality and peace, but in truth I am the absurd, the destroyer of internal cultural and political unity of my kind, for the destroyers of humanity)?
Who am I today? Where do I reside in the minds of today's dark faces that I have betrayed yesterday on into these days of Prison Industrial Complex, Global Warming, CIA Wars of Toppling Peoples' Governments, and reassuring Master Clinton and Gates, Master Greenspan and the Federal Reserve, Master Rothschild and the Trilateral Commission that the darkies are in check, selfcheck? Who am I? Am I the Negro in amerikkkan politics, a dictator of Ghana, the school teacher in some public school? I am lost, for I can now see the pain that I have caused, but I refuse to change! For I do have an inter-

est in the unjust order that controls today! My house, my cars, my women, my trips to the Virgin Islands each summer and fall!...I know that I am the lower half of the self that makes waste of the godman called Afrikan. I am the worst part of this Afrikanlife. But for the sake of change and the continuation of existence, I will have to stop fighting my higher self, the illumination of god in all humanity! But she loves me more than watching the pulverizing effects of that industrial and corporate waste has on the ecosystem! I, the cowardly man, know that I am the confusion that causes this brave heart and TRU man to stumble about, through this vortex, this matrix of visions of better days to come and the ways and means of becoming more man than rebel! Though I am torn, I have a choice! I am weak, but seem to love it!

I am the self-interest motivated coward; the lower half of the higher self.

VI

Raising himself back to his constant state of self, he cringes at the malignant cowardice he just witnessed within himself. His descent into the hell of self has left him weak and feeble minded. This vulgar half of our warrior has made its presence known to him. He looks to the stars of his mind. He contemplates his entire being in an attempt to understand the source of this part of him that loves the malignant ways of Mary. This contemplation gives life to the light of understanding. His understanding is grown greater. The power which his lower self possesses is only possible for as long as he allows himself to submit to the absurdity and grotesque pleasure of she who holds the power of death in her mind, heart, and hands. Swimming his way to the island of forgotten bliss, he thinks of the strength he will need to prepare himself for the coming struggle with himself. That the true foe is not the she-devil, but himself, is quite clear to him after his descent into himself. She has been only able to do as much as he has allowed her to do to him. Having reached the shores of forgotten bliss, he seeks out the virgins of tomorrow, locating them, he stands erect for their healing powers of truth and innocence to disburden him of the misery.

Feeling regenerated, moving forth with an antiquated concept of resistance ingrained into his intellect, he attempts to leap into the arms of revolution. Into the arms of a place inside himself where the love of self and kind can never be destroyed. He sought that which could not be expressed in dialogue or song; he sought out the eternally expressed thought of the incessant desire to be a part and partial of all of the essence and beauty of that which is absent from the materialistic concept of history pushed by the open foe of the gods and man. Pushing one hundred and thirty-five years, determined to live as a warrior, sane and committed, should, and in spite of the coward that resides within the carnal realm of his mind, he struggles to be free. The time of walking down the middle road of this life has come to an end—there is to be no more straddling of the fence. No matter the temptation, no matter how overwhelming the desire, he has fixed his resolve on his mission to become much more than a pawn, a willing slave in this battle between godman and the idea of Satan personified in the person of capitalist man. No more excuse, no more lies, no more illusions as to who the foe is. The principles of love and life must override that of the foe's precepts pushed by the likes of Rikki Lake and Bill Cosby...

"Alas, so he proclaims it thus so! Seeing is believing. Well, to be more precise, in this case, being is the determining factor of it all." So saith, with much doubt, the Higher Half of this suffering human being.

VII

The cool air of a fan blows into his sweaty face as he attempts to rest in a prison cell. He closes his eyes and for the third time he tries to block out the din of noise that assaults his sanity. Like the sound of a coming swarm of killer bees, the voices of the dispossessed grind away at his last nerve, but he does not reply in kind with his justified and righteous rage at the ignorance and idiocy of the noise makers. Talk of football, Emmett Smith scoring a touch down, and the ranting and raving of all the Redskins fans, is the deepest these captives can get. Nothing concerning their future or the fascist practices of their keepers is even uttered let alone discussed. The process of leaving the duty and responsibility of one's existence in the hands of another ultimately leads to dull minds, sore backs, body counts, and early graves. The descent into the obvious political and cultural grave continues on into the next generation, on into the coming of the new lord. These abject fools, these victims of the Mary, long to be free only to be made the slaves of a different kind. Given up the promise of the coming of the lord, for a few moments of fettered glory, they all sing:

O, stand the storm, it won't be long
We'll anchor bye and bye, O Brethren!
Stand the storm, it won't be long,
We'll anchor bye and bye.

This was the cry of, the song wailed by, those of our kind as they traveled the middle roads of never can never return home again in their life time. Carrying the burden of the forecoming storm, the leap into the open mouth of Amerikkka, swallowed whole, eaten by the greedy little children of the bastard race of the she-devil. The puppies of the she-devil were the parasitic discharge of a land without any worth, with no ability to support the greed and cowardice of a seething species bent on stupid. Honesty, trust, and love are things that these wolves have not the capacity to display without malice—yesterday or today. They gather and travel in great numbers only because of their delusional fear of termination by the gods. Carrying on in the name of liberty and justice, singing the blues of Muddy Waters, the children of the gods find life in chains unbearable. In spite of the fact that a great many of them wear the face of happiness while in the chains of fine clothes, affirmative action, the uniforms of their colonial masters, as they sing with Hitler the happy tunes of the Chi-lites, Blue Magic, and Michael Jackson—wishing to god that Thug Life was dead! Why! Cause it reminds them of the things that they would like to forget. Times and days filled with the Black Power, BLA, BPP, NALF, Fred Hampton, George and Jon Jackson, Tupac Shakur, and a New Afrikan tomorrow...And still our hero is but a coward!

VIII

In a box surrounded by mud, he was dead. As he looked over the flat plains of tomorrows to come, he thought of the visions he had of digging his way out of this hell of lost time, forgotten history, and crazed niggas. Maddened by the remembering of the mountains shoved in his path by the hands of socialism; the hands of Marx and Lenin. The marxism he read told him of the evil of narrow nationalism; while (as he was to find out much later) the marxists who wrote the stuff were very nationalist, very proud and assured of their "Father Land's" place in the sun...He thought of New Afrika, a Black Father Land in amerika. But, still not wanting to emerge from the daze of having supposed to be slain, he floats down the throat of the beast. With Motown sounds, daring rays of gospel hope, and civil rights lies engrossing his mind, he got lost in the pictures of his childhood. The man in a box surrounded by mud, still trying to evade the she-devil, looked through the photo album of mind; back to the day when his innocence was lost forever. Meeting the She-Devil for the first time, through the action of a savage bent on possessing that which wasn't his; he fought and slew, in a child's way, the opponent who dared trespass on property that wasn't his. Over some girl. On this day, in this picture memory, he felt for the first time the rational killing passion of jealousy. He raged on some fool, Tod, who dared to move in on his little girlfriend. They both were about the same age, his opponent was a bit taller and heavier, but he was simply a bit more fatal than Tod was mentally. The trespasser kissed his first piece, felt her little titties, and tried to put his middle finger where it shouldn't have gone. She ran to him crying, he reacted in a quiet and determined manner, and with a patience only a child of his breed could.

He waited until a few days passed, saw his chance when the wrongdoer was playing some childish game involving cardboard boxes they found in the parking lot of the local supermarket. They were playing racing cars by placing the boxes over their heads, making the sounds of cars, moving over the well kept lawn of the soon to be victim's backyard. He watched Tod with great keenness, and once the box went over his head, the jealousy-filled child ran, full speed, towards his foe. Smashing full force into the box-covered fool, whose head slammed with great impact on the protruding water spigot (used to water the lawn)...Blood, screams, and tears came from his foe...Smiles, inner laughing, and debased pleasure was all that was felt by the child conquistador. Though the sun was up, with the sweet smell of freshly cut grass in the air, the gloom that overtook the mind of the children who witnessed his action blocked out the day's paradise-like life giving rays. In the mind of the child within the man, it connected his actions with the violent actions he witnessed his father commit against the men who slept with his mother. The correlation brought to bear by a child who thought the savage killing of JoJo, by a man who found him in bed with his woman, was thought to be the manner in which right was determined. He felt proud of himself, he felt like all thug niggas must have felt after tasting their first drop of blood, after experiencing their first rite of passage via the attempt to push a violator out of existence. He felt strong.

Closing the picture album of his mind, with a start, he opened his eyes and reflected on that long forgotten memory, that defining moment in his breeding, that instant where he had begun to accept his role, his status, as slave and nigga. He thought of the bitch that was in constant pursuit of his soul. He thought that maybe she did own him; that maybe his attempt to resist her will was all in vain? That maybe at the age of nine she was successful at plaguing and bending his soul to her way of life? He thought that maybe he was crazy; that he had crossed over into the hellish utopia of "Alice in Wonderland"—a fairy tale land created by a madman, a sick man; a land wherein the weak and defeated retreated when they have decided that they can no longer stand the insanity of an absurd reality made to appear to be the normality of all possible existence. After all, he was hiding out from her in a prison cell!

IX

Was it an idea that was in pursuit of the bent and twisted mind of this man, who has sadly grown accustomed to the abuse and misuse of his very existence for the sake of others' dominant bent and twisted conceptualization of life? Did he dare assume that this force, this power made manifest, that hunted and haunted his dreams and thoughts, his every waking moment and aspired ambition to be free, was the embodiment of that place wherein he was born, and made to worship as if it was unreproachable? Was the she-devil an idea? Was it a world-view that plagued his center because it was alien and profane? No thought of relief, no promise of release, from the grips of an ethos that has convinced the world of its god ordered and universal application, was in sight for this sad soul, this child of poverty and despair, who had dared question the basic assumptions of this beast's right to brand him "SLAVE", the property of the USA. There was to be no release from the grips of this cultural matrix that has unleashed the worse in man onto the beauty of a world designed to guide and direct its own course. He was sure to have to finally seek relief at the end of a rope, the drawn guns of the hired hands of the state, at the end of the road of misplaced hate.

He had attempted with all of his might, his will, to seek the absurdity of all that was called normal; but his attempts were of no use—so it

A DISJOINTED SEARCH FOR THE WILL TO LIVE

seemed to him. "Give the fuck up!" cried his debased self, his defeated self. "Hold on, be strong!" were the cries of his ancestors. He tried to remember himself a boy; he tried to remember a time when he considered himself to be braveheart and tru! Finding that he had in his mind's eye the beginning images of something from the past, he focused all of his attention on the image; as he sat cross-legged upon a shelf, in a box atop the empire state building, with a girl named daze-ee singing him to sleep—just as the image of the past came looming, full force, into focus. He remembered; and then, he affirmed:

The struggle,
this war of
wear and tear,
demands that we
drink the sweet
blood of communion
of the heart
and mind,
love and care,
trust and faith
for we ourselves
alone
in the just
and undying
cause of life
over death,
us over
them!

PART TWO

I

In Charm City, USA, Kenny, TC, and me were on our way to do a little boosting at the local Kmart. Walking along the sun baked sidewalk of some busy street lined with abandoned homes. Houses that were in such a state of emptiness for as far back as I could remember. Laughing, telling jokes, without a care in the world, we performed the walk of young panthers, minus the noiselessness of our fathers; a walk possessed by proud youth who were assured of their innate greatness, in spite of their unconsciousness of the incorruptible significance and purpose of that greatness. We were just a couple of Richard Wright "Black Boys", from the caste of the untouchables, hooking school on a warm Juneteenth day. Inhaling, exhaling, the deadly exhaust of passing cars filled with pale folk who viewed us with much contempt, mixed with hidden dark Freudian sex fantasies carried out in back streets, dark hallways, and porno movie playing television filled motel rooms. We just smiled at them knowingly, keeping their hatred and longing to ourselves. There were more exciting things for us to think about and do this Juneteenth day; a day on which our kin folk of old received the belated news of their supposed freedom. Having just completed our hustles with the can and bottle collecting, pumping gas at the Exxon station, and, finally, washing car windows at the intersection of North and Gay St., we were looking forward to getting high off of whatever our pocket's full of nickels and quarters and dimes, with a few dollar bills, could buy us. We felt, and were thinking each in our own minds, that we were rich, ghetto child rich.

A DISJOINTED SEARCH FOR THE WILL TO LIVE

When, without rhyme or reason, my senses slowed down to the surreal pace of the ticking secondhand of the clock in last period class, home economics. Yet none of what I was experiencing had anything to do with some school boy's boredom psychosis. In the present state that my body existed in, functioned in, and that I was conscious of up until that moment, ceased to be, and the dreamlike condition was all that I was experiencing. I looked around at my homies, looking to see if their senses were tasting the same thing as I. TC looked as if he was telling some sort of joke, as he was making some weird face, while baring his gold teeth. I attempted to speak, but my lips took forever and a lightyear to release the words that held the thoughts which I was attempting to share with them; words, which if released, would have informed them of this weird shit that had my ass seeing, hearing, tasting, smelling, and feeling in slow motion. They just went on laughing, telling jokes, without as much as showing a hint of awareness of my absence of participation in the art of "bullshittin' around", without a care in the world, as usual. They continued to move along the Ave., without taking note of my state nor the fact that I no longer traveled with them. Though I was quite scared, I was sort of amused at the coolness and balmy feelings that were now the dominant sensations that moved throughout my being—sensations that were quite alien to my old yet young sensibilities. It was these alien sensations that overruled that familiar urge to retreat, and at this development, I laughed aloud, and I heard not my laugh. "What the fuck is this shit!" were the only words I could utter for quite some time.

I began to smell and taste cotton candy and popcorn, accompanied by a tantalizing feeling, violently stirring in my belly, of palm trees and white sand, moving throughout my body. Coming to rest at my core, an unidentified experience of a thirst and passion for life was spelled out clearly there at my center. Without forewarning, these sensations were touched up, enhanced, by the colorful images of past life made to appear in the present realm of "never can never say never." The colorful images of Woodstock, of Jimi Hendrix in a Nike sweatsuit, with

"The Rose" on his arm, sporting a g-string. Now I was really scared! Thinking to myself, "Now I am seeing dead people sing dance, and perform lewd sex acts." Petrified as could be, I stopped and turned to face a badly painted gray house, with a lone and motionless figure sitting upon its chipped marble steps, in the shadows. As I attempted to focus my eyes in on this lone figure, that sat without a hint of life, I was remembering that nickel bag of weed I smoked behind the dumpsite, in the alley, behind the Gay St. Jewish Cutrate, before stopping off at TC's house—to wake his lazy ass up as always. Hoping and praying that I was hallucinating, and hadn't gone plain cuckoo. I stated to myself, "That shit had to be laced with something as bad as me." But the thought of weed just really wasn't enough to convince me that all I was then experiencing was connected with it. "Fuck it!" I said aloud to myself, while ignoring the motionless figure, "I'm just gonna let this shit roll me along to whatever destiny it brings me to…I ain't no fuckin ho, no fuckin chump, no fuckin sucker! I can deal with this crazy shit!" Having no idea why I was speaking such brave words, in such an odd world, I just simply returned my attention back to the oddly familiar aloneness that sat before me.

Focusing my eyes in on the lone figure that sat in the shadows on the chipped marble stoops of the six eyed, three story, gray painted skin spilling house, an image began to emerge through the haze of pink and gray, and I began to make out that the lone figure was a girl. "Alas!" Before me, now in full delusional focus, wearing a pink flowered summer dress, sat a brown complexioned, dreadlocked, bright eyed Nubian; with lips so full, so voluptuous, that my heart did something new; it danced for this strange girl. With the sunlight brightly, without warning, shining its crayon yellow rays on the unforgettable portrait of this girl of TRU beauty; of a beauty that consecrated my entire being beyond the crumbling demise of my unholy ghetto logic—a logic shoved there, in my head, by the beast who sat in some cesspool of greed called the white corporation. With a light breeze blowing through her locks, I smiled with the scent of summertime bloom mov-

A DISJOINTED SEARCH FOR THE WILL TO LIVE | 26

ing in and out of my surreal hypersensitive olfactory sense organ. With great surprise I realized that my nose no longer picked up the ill aromas of the toxic fumes being emitted from the dreaded streets full of western man's passing oxygen killing machines.

A million centuries removed from the ugly "Business As Usual" world full of decadence and decay, I was, thankfully, in a surreal world, which was bringing to my six senses much joy and confusion. I noticed that she was smiling, but I knew not why. I had to close my eyes to cut the flow of tears of joy and confusion. Without opening them, I saw her slowly stand and float towards me. With a light breeze pushing her pink flowered dress close to her firm body, displaying to my eyes a shape that was mouth watering and exceptionally radiant; a form out of this world comely. Having no further desire to shed tears, being moved to take note of this living reality removed from the ugliness, the objectification of glossy Covergirl, Sports Illustrated, Hustler magazine covers, I shouted out in my own words: "She be the bomb, forreal." Having shouted such an affirmation of something greater, I felt as if I was being removed from my skin, my body, my deformed sanity. Yet, without fear of this intense and strange feeling, still I was smiling the smile of the TRU sphinx before the perverting kiss of Napoleon's prejudiced cannon violently removed its nose, its lips, my nose and lips, the nose and lips of the true children of Afrikan genius.

Without uttering a word, she moved, walked, or floated to me. Touching my face with her lips, while looking me in the eyes, tasting my weed high, saying nothing. I felt her lips quiver, and suddenly I was transported to a room empty of the gloom of my own; a room full of pretty things, shining things, and there she sat with a book bearing the title "I Ching" laying in her lap. Smiling, I floated over to her, kneeling at her feet, taking her hand in my own, bringing them up to my lips, without speaking, I kissed them, while looking into her eyes and smelling her scent of life before the death of passion in the hearts and minds of men. I sat at her feet as she read to me from "The Book of

Change", and I somehow understood the complex, yet simple, concepts and precepts of the book that spoke through her to me. We then danced to music that I had no idea existed—music without sound or words. She said that her name was Summer, without moving her lips or uttering a word—come to think about it, she performed the same masterstroke with the reading of the book. No words were ever spoken. We just enjoyed each other's being; just being human, man-child to woman-child.

Removing her quivering lips from my cheek, she held my stare with her own, as I found myself standing wide-eyed before her, smiling as if I had just eaten of the forbidden and hidden reality of the mode of life which is denied in the world outside of this surreal one that she and I shared. She informed me that she was of this world, the one that existed, that progressed and decayed, all at once, all around us, outside of our surreal heavenly sublime one. She too was a ghetto child, her time was spent between school and watching her younger brothers and sisters, her father was locked-down in some concentration camp (as was my old dad), and her mother was a neurotic, sexually repressed jesus freak—as was mine. We had a great deal in common, though we lived so far apart, in different cities, states, and countries. She spoke a different language, which I somehow could understand. Sao Paulo, Brazil is where she hailed from.

She shared with me the nature of the blatant and latent forms of white supremacy that plagues the country that her ancestors were brought to in chains; she told me of how, because her skin is dark, she is made to feel less than human by an unjust order bent on creating the perfect white society—the code word for this thrust is the colorless society, the society where racism and injustice will not exist; for all the niggas will be died and gone...She spoke of things concerning what she called "genocide" through politics, culture, and other things which she learned through reading books and studying her lived experiences. She told me of the police death squads that went through the streets, in the downtown business districts, murdering homeless and mentally ill children of Afrikan descent. I cringed at the images of the twisted wasted youth, and the inhuman behavior of the fascists that committed such deeds in the name of the capitalist. I mourned, and knew not why.

After she shared, I began to express aspects of my life's suffering and hardship that I had no idea were real; and I had no idea that these realities where blighted economic and social arrangements that were/are imposed on me and mine from forces outside of our communities (so-called ghettos) for greed and genocide. Without warning, I began to scream! In a rage, I cursed the very thing that had begun to open my eyes to the ugly realities of my life, of the valuelessness of my very existence. I dared not look into my own heart for fear of affirming the dominant culture's assumptions of my soulless and savage state. Was I capable of life beyond the hell of this existence as a young nigga, a social waste, a nonentity living off the crumbs and mercy of those good christian white folk down at the Salvation Army's nigga killin' churches of self-determination destroying doctrine of "give the niggas bread and second hand clothes, and they will give you their hearts and souls, and the information necessary to kill that revolutionary potential, that essential Afrikan and genetic cultural memory, that natural inclination for life and self-determination, that longs to be released against that which has been denying them their rights to life, liberty and the pursuit of happiness since before the mistake called Columbus."

And just as fast as this explosion of fear, rage, and agony began, it ended. And I felt as if I had something to live for! Something to Love and Struggle for, as an Afrikan man-child with love for himself and his kind over the delusional and imposed love of the amerikkkan thing, the amerikkkan "I had a dream" lie told to millions of hopeful and believing men, women, and children and Dr. King! A dream that involved the selling of one's soul and being trained, through a depraved sociopathic, economically unjust, intellectually and morally bankrupt socialization process, how to come to unnaturally hate the subtle levels of life, the essence of life—the very earth that one walked on. For Love and Struggle, the beauty of life, I felt the surge of resistance to all that the Bill Clintons of the world were pushing for: the completion of the "New World Order" paradigm...But I was taken aback, I tried to release myself from her all-consuming gaze, but she would not let me go. The images I began to encounter of life and struggle, of what these two concepts would mean to me, compelled me to laugh and cry, to hope and despair, to take heart and to be scared.

I pleaded with Summer to let me go, but her only reply was to smile...but, somehow, I understood why all this was occurring, yet I didn't dare attempt to accept this large responsibility, my kind's historical duty the world over. But still I would like to know, what is this surreal feeling of reality all about? Why is it that my heart beats slow songs of love and struggle, in spite of the fact that my third eye witnesses the hardship of taking, practicing, and maintaining such a life, such a world-view?...My thoughts moved to the essence I had come to know as Summer, questioning further the absurd possibility of her and I. Why the brightness shone in her eyes, the radiance of her smile, all seems to inject into my heart, my soul, a bit of that which I have yet come to know, to feel? Was this sort of love possible? If I were to touch her back in the blighted world where my body stood, would I cry from the sheer joy of it? If I were to kiss her sugar brown face, her perfect full lips, would I witness shooting stars going off somewhere in my head? And from somewhere in the heavens of my soul, an angelic knowing voice whispered to me: You, my child of hardship and longing, shall one day know that all of this is so, if any of this is possible. For she will be yours and you hers...Smiling a soul smile at this prophecy, I thanked the whisper.

And the thought: *that which has been image need not be forgotten* rang throughout my being. Summer danced to this shout, this chanti-

A DISJOINTED SEARCH FOR THE WILL TO LIVE | 30

ng, that was being played through to her from me, and from her back to me again. We both danced like long lost friends, though in reality we were two newly wedded souls. We became intertwined in an embrace of life over the death of the world which we would have to soon return to; understanding that we wouldn't be allowed to carry the full memory of this experience; understanding that it was we who had to suffer the insufferable abuse of a world gone mad—a world bent on its own destruction, its own demise. We did not despair, we laughed and sang the words: "That which has been imaged needed not be forgotten!" Dancing to the swinging tones of the Yardbird, Charlie Parker, rapped the "Nigga Blues" with Tupac...walking the Ho Chi Minh Trail with Amilcar Cabral, taking note of the victorious struggle of a proud and brave people...Not daring to care about the might of the foe which we had to return home to confront and fight, as we did hope and pray to one day rid the world of this archfiend. No tears is to be shed at our journey's end. "We must build to win," I heard some old yet young Black Panther sing to us both; a Paanther of the Brave Heart and TRU, Chairman Newton, breed of BLACK CAT! Spending this night, our first and last, rolling about on the floor of the collective memory of glory days and Marcus Garvey parades. We made love; knowing all the while that we would one day be free to do such things in the other, outer world of the earthland that screamed for our return; our return back to the mission that the she-devil prayed us to fail at.

Kissing my sweet Summer goodbye, not forever, but only for a time. "Every goodbye ain't gone; every big man ain't strong!" We said, in unspoken words, that our love would remain, that we would meet again in the world that we both dreaded having to return to. Saying I love you, at once, without crying, we both were back to where we began—in our respective colonial homes of nigga hate and white death. Crying the tears of heart wrenching loss; trying to convince myself to let the tears flow without fear or concern for the thoughts or verbalized opinions of the passing B-Boys, Thugs, and Drug Hustlers. I walked home. Finding TC sitting upon the steps of my house, nodding and scratching from the poison he didn't want to share with me; totally oblivious of my state, let alone the fact that I had passed him by, leaving him to enjoy his escape, his 20 minute vacation, away from the decaying lot of Black Life.

Entering my momma's house, I slowly found my way to my bedroom. Upon finding my frameless mattress, my bed without springs, me and my heavy heart dropped off to the natural escape to be found via REM sleep. Going under. Going, going, going, gone!

II

Brave Heart

Awakening to find himself still deep in REM slumber, not wanting to return to the scattered world of a displaced people, who once carried the names of a proud and industrious people—a civilized people. In REM mode, he finds himself still without a name to be proud of…Kneegrow, black, Afro, or jungle bunny, weren't names that he felt any particular sort of kinship to or with. He still felt weak and broken in two. Separated from himself, his kind, and the other half of humanity, in this REM state he attempted to construct and relive some past noble experience of resistance to that bitch, that idea that was given life to by he who has created a world that consumes itself, a world order that is determined to generate, accumulate, and consume the material resources of shit that ain't theirs to enjoy. It is in such a world that he has been chained, and it seems it is only through escapist methods that he is capable of reliving the greatness of his past lives. So, in here, in this REM state, he proclaims and remembers the times, "When I was young I thought myself to be a 'Valiant Warrior'":

In some big city residential/business district, I lurked through a parking lot full of unoccupied cars—which I assumed were abandoned under the cover of a moonless, star-dotted night time sky. Looking to expropriate a radio or two, loose change, or anything valuable that I carry away and sell hot to the junkyard boys out in Bowie, MD. With bowie knife in hand—which served as both defense weapon and tool of crude removal—I tried the doors of each car I passed, with a feeling of great adventure and intrigue flooding my every nerve ending. Without making a sound, I moved over the broken glass, empty beer cans, and other assorted trash, without making as much as a rustle of noise.

In these times I had no need to worry too much about car alarms, motion detectors, or any other sort of contraption, and should I have come across a car or truck with one, I would simply take flight like a swift chicken hawk. I would make like my favorite heroes in all the western movies, the so-called Indians, and make like a jack rabbit running for the hills; escaping the evil bite of the guns of John Wayne and Clint Eastwood. Only to return another day, for protracted warfare, when the settlers are all gluttonously enjoying that which isn't theirs.

Without no alarms, guards, or any other fascist devices designed to protect the stolen property of the rich; without worry, and with ease, I had secured a radio with cassette player, one bottle of Jack Daniels, and a couple cases of 45 shells. As I was moving in on my eighth car, my eyes came across the emblem of the empire: The Stars and Stripes; the blood soaked red, white, and blue. "Shit! I'm gonna go to jail!" I thought out loud, in a strained whisper, with more than a hint of fear resonating in my words. "These cops gonna pull my damn finger prints up off these fuckin' cars! That's all I need...fuck 'em!" I thought and said out loud—with a shout. With knife in hand, without thought or remorse, I proceeded to cut and stab each tire of every car on that lot. Taking great pleasure in this action that somehow relieved me of the pressure of the coming storm, the coming confrontation between she and I who have been in constant battle since before I was born into this body of a child, in this society patterned after all of the founding fathers' greatest freak fantasies of LAW AND ORDER, WHIPS AND

CHAINS, AND PAIN AND NO SANE SOCIETY WOULD DARE BUCK THE COMING OF THE DAY WHEN THE RICH WOULD NOT HAVE TO WORRY ABOUT DYING AT THE HANDS OF SOME FOUL LITTLE NIGGA SUCH AS ME! I would be too busy killing folk that suffered as I did, not talking of Marcus Garvey days, self determination, human rights, or reparations for the 400 centuries of building up the wealth of the insane society that would begin shoving me in a cage at 13 years of age. Because of the harm it had caused me since before I was born in 1984, drove me to kill that which I hated equally to myself—that nigga that looked as I did. Though still, at that moment when I felt free to strike out at the property of the state, I attempted to entertain thoughts of these actions in the parking lot like such actions that were carried out against the invaders from the north, back in the old days when pride and hope still flowed and surged openly in the hearts and minds of my kind.

Just like the old days, these valiant actions against the foe who sought to make my kind simple expendable pawns in his game of capital gain and lost souls, touched off within me the soaring experience of courageous elation, sanity and love. With the use of such a resilient remembrance of such unsung days and times, my dreaming consciousness turns the control of the dream over to the unconscious, to my soul, and I become the Bugandan general that I once was. They called me Kabaka Mutesa I, the divine ruler of the nation-state of Buganda—now called Uganda by my children who remember me not; my children who follow after the gods of the palemen of europe—the very men that have razed the once great and vast beauty of their homeland. Though I had the heart of a lion and the innate intellect to guide and govern my people, this paleman thought we Bugandians unworthy of the right to live as a free and self-determining people. The so-called great explorer and discoverer, Henry Morton Stanley, wrote his culturally imperialistic opinion about me: "I saw that he was highly clever and possessed of the ability to govern, but his cleverness and ability lacked the mannerisms of a European's."

He wrote these debasing and anti-human remarks though I had treated him as a man, a human being, and allowed him to pass through our country secure in his person. In spite of the normal and proper functioning of our economy, of our society, of our manner of government, he called us savage and godless—in the light of history, it is he and his kind who have no god. Though he called me "Your Highness" to my face, speaking in a most humble and respectful manner, he still wrote home to his king, calling me nigger, plotting to destroy our way of life and rob us of our Homeland, though we fed and protected him and his men. (Our First and Last Mistake!): "Oh for the hour when a band of philanthropic capitalists shall vow to rescue these beautiful lands, and supply the means to enable the Gospel messengers to come and quench the murderous hate with which man beholds the beautiful lands around Lake Victoria!"

They left with our trust and respect. And the hour came when they returned to expropriate our land, our homes, our children, our way of life from out of our very hands; and we were not prepared for the murderous hate unleashed on our beloved people and the demented rape of our beautiful homeland by spiritless savages who hailed from the polar regions; who in the name of their gods did us and humanity an insufferable and grave injustice. But his god, capitalism, allows for such atrocities; justifies such inhumanity. It is good that those who went before us, our ancestors, did not have to witness the coming of the she-devil, the pale scourge of humanity. It is good that I do not have to live through that which "he who dreams himself me" has to endure, survive, and attempt to thrive in—the world created by he who has made a sacrilege of the history of all that was once the closest to the fulfilling of humanity's search for humanity. It is good that those who went before us, our anscestors, did not have to witness the coming of the she-devil, the demon lover of death and masked smiles of santa maria, the pale scourge of humanity...It is good that I am not alive to see, to live in, the diabolical, unfeeling, and anti-human world that he who remembers himself me, he who possesses resilient remembrance, he who dreams this nightmare, now has to live in as but a flicker of the "great people" we once were.

III

There was no happiness nowhere to be found in this life of unvalue, this life that had been devalued a million times in one life time, from the womb to the culture death: abortion, the death penalty, projects, thug life, middle class, bill gates billionaire dreams of state pen, wage slavery, sweat shop, Bigmac clown fame. No happiness to be spoken of, all the smiles that he smiled were smiles that reflected the illusions and broken dreams; internet sex and down-sizing the government, murder of social responsibility. From chained feet to chained hands; from long boat rides to the promise of a better life after he died. The collective suffering, the unified demise, was all a part of the grand design. With speechless intent, he could do nothing but dream and remember the pain of heavenly lies and debased running around the world of bullshit in the park, walking dogs, and chasing big butt freaks for a "I am going to fuck you for the sake of hating you, bitch!", in the name of being a true reflection of a weak man in the cloth of grand schemes of being a player: a destroyer of the beauty of womanhood, a rejecter of the life to be had by she who loved me more than life and tomorrow.

He remembered that there was no happiness nowhere to be found in this life of his unvalue; he remembered devalued existence in this place of Amerikkkan dreams fulfilled for the few. He remembered locked doors, cuffed hands, his hands, well he sat before that very locked door, attempting to escape the torture of a demented victim of the Amerikkkan dream…and he remembered the morbid life line of unvalue, devalued existence in a place that only saw him as a threat,
though
he was but

a child in
a dirty pamper:
"Locked behind a wood framed door."

IV

Locked behind a wood framed screen door, my hands in handcuffs, I sit on the cold, dirty floor I have learned to share with the roaches. As thoughts of how to remove the painfully tight and restrictive shiny handcuffs placed on my wrist by my angry stepfather (for committing some wrong that I was unaware of; a wrong that I did not remember committing), I thought of freedom. Thoughts of freedom ran through my mind, through my tear-filled eyes, as I viewed the world through the locked screen door. I tasted the snot that ran from my runny nose. With my fettered hands, with my eyes locked on the world outside of the screen door, I reached for the door knob, placing my tiny hands on it. I turned, but it would not move. I began to feel a need to be away from that place...with tears of confusion streaming from my eyes, I looked at the world outside of the locked screen door, heard it calling to me. Suddenly my baby brown eyes locked on a big yellow light in the sky...momma called it the sun...I watched it as it went away, out of the sky, wondering to myself: "Why?"...broken bones need mending, scarred souls need healing!

Now I sit on a hard unmade bed, locked behind equally hard steel bars, confined in a cold and dirty cell with roaches I talk to—living creatures with whom I have dialogued about the relevance of theirs and my own existence. With my freedom far out beyond these bars, walls, razor wire, and gun towers, I think of that very freedom that had been unjustly taken away from me, so many years ago. I think of the shackles, the strip searches, the count times, the chow lines, the knife fights, the comrades that have died in this hell though they had not committed any crimes—though they were innocent men whose only crimes were being born New Afrikan and surviving...broken bones need mending, scarred souls need healing!

Here I sit, cross-legged like a Buddha, reflecting on the image of that five year old child in chains; thinking of the pain and trauma that such a dastardly deed had opened up within that child's little mind, and I cry the tears of a man who now understands what that child also understood then; in spite of the cruelty of such a world, he and I must continue to fight for our freedom, never giving in to the criminals who have profited from the physical demise of our liberty, and the almost complete destruction of our ability to become much more than what this system was/is designed to shape and mold our kind into...beast of burden, sub-human drones, the floor mat of white supremacy. Never will we give up until freedom is won—freedom from fear, freedom from malicious uncertainty, freedom from the adversarial reality created by our enemies, the enemies of humanity...broken bones need mending, scarred souls need healing!

Here I sit, as I sat all those years ago, as that child who looked into the setting sun and saw freedom. Here I sit watching the sun within my heart and soul, knowing as I knew then that I would be free, that I would be much more than what my step-father was; knowing that I would never submit to the dehumanizing forces that sought to make me just another broken nigga gone unmended...just another scarred nigga gone unhealed...So, today, right at this moment, with the inner calm and resolve of the cross-legged revolutionary...into my inner setting sun I look, understanding that this unjust confinement I now suffer, and must endure, will one day end; knowing that I will greet tomorrow's rising sun in freedom's loving embrace, full of warmth and grace. Smiling the smile of he who had begun and completed the epic journey of a thousand miles.

I am broken bones that have mended,
a scarred soul that has healed.

A DISJOINTED SEARCH FOR THE WILL TO LIVE 38

And thus must we all struggle to help
mend and heal each other…
daily, yearly, until all are free!

Just locked doors and broken spirits was all he thought of; lost in a trail of tears, masks, glossed over by the bullshit of the amerikkkan mistake of equality and a level playing field. He went to the holidays spent behind the safety net of white folk smoking dope, playing at being thugs, never caring to know what it was all about. They called it hip hop, but it was really black life being snuffed out, denied, and rejected by an order that could only exist at the expense of these helpless souls, the victim of history written and pushed by those who valued and dominated the scene of the coming of Cataclysm.

V

A Cataclysm that read like the book of revelation written in the year 2000:

The smile of a child at odious play in the halls of the White House. The laugh of mom with dad, in a porno movie. The joy of love gained and adversity conquered. The heart-felt need of tomorrow's solace, and the TRU heart courage and Nat Turner vision to make solace actual. Speed balling, running and skipping to the beat of the sun dyed sky, with the scent of the pine trees of this enchanted promise, in a land long thought dead, in a time long forgotten, you move down a path paved with typing paper and pepsi cans, searching for the place called home—a forest where tigers are plant eaters and deers are tiger chasers.

Bellowing to the drunk robins and maced blue jays to start a group and sing for the children fighting and shooting dope over by the jungle gym, in the school yard, on the playground. Where the girls and boys are turning tricks, for weed smoke, on swings and seesaws. Dancing to the distant rhythm of the ocean on a beach where dead turtles are large enough to ride, where the dodo birds still come to feed right out of your hands, making their laughable walk to receive their reward for still being nonexistant in this Graceland built for King Elvis.

Touched by an angel, which lives among the stars, that whispers in the wind the coming of the lord, in your ear, on a surf board with nauseating wings—deformed by the industrial waste from a plant that was but a mile from its nest. Remembering the year when the storm of Noah came to carry away all the mean and bad folk of the day—the Yuppies and Slumlords. Riding off into the setting sun of the east, in some sort of ship built with orange peels and apple seeds and held together with the dung of inmates from the state prisons and asylums—who were left behind because of their fanatical and just cry for "The Rights of Woman and Man." Trying to find that land where the storm, brought on by the mean and bad sons of man, could not reach. When suddenly the ship of orange peels and apple seeds began to grow trees that bore the fruit of better days to come—the offspring of the children of the ghettos; the children of messy sex and 2pac rap songs full of hope and prayer for the existence of such a place being in a heaven somewhere—that somewhere being a better ghetto than the ones left behind.

In the desert, under which lay a city of old, you walked with a green monkey that talked of revolution, wars of liberation, and international upheaval. A monkey that smelled of fish oil and turkey gravy. You walking as if you were in some enchanted forest. It is 125 degrees, but in the shadows of the Empire State building you spot an oasis—a product of your need. You say to the talkative monkey, "See you that oasis over there a pace? Smell you that memory-stirring sweet scent of womanhood and ice cream soda—reminiscent of 1986?" The monkey, though, pays you no mind as he continues to forecast the end of the world—while drooling MTV and Sega. In the cool flowing spring are nude men and women in mental belts, spawned from computer chips designed and produced in the European Union. Actually the labor of the slaves from the colonies put these Virtual Reality contraptions together. This witless mass of wealthy gray folk pay you two no never mind—too engrossed in their mind programs of whips and chains, leather spankings and Debbie Does Everybody videos; they call these extreme sports. You both now nude, now bathing, still talking. Correction! The green monkey continues his timeworn discourse of international tragedy and the end of capitalist man and his bubble gum system of soda pop, cool beer, slick cars, noiseless jet planes and politics of cowardly cravens. Yet he says nothing of the 21st century colonies in the Amerikas, Asia, Europe, Afrika. You leave this place. Flying away from the green monkey that sounded like the defunct Weather Underground, with much words and guns, but no practice or gunpowder, you shed a tear for the calamity that still befalls your kind and have a lighthearted laugh for the days to come—dancing in the street, inhaling tru oxygen unbefouled by the dead and gone metropolis.

Aye, but the irresistible voices of Karin Uhoh and Alaina Daddy O brings you to a stop at a planet called earth. Their flamingo pink lips, covered in Victoria's Secret red, whisper the desires of the sons of man to you, and to the evil paradise you arrive. Earth, that old crept of a prison, of the mind and spirits, over the people that dwell there. What a horrid place it be. Earth that turning, spinning globe of water and clouds, with a molten hot core, with cold-hearted gray people, has become a different place since last you had cared to visit. What is this you see? People actually loving people! This has to be but a ridiculous dream! An optical illusion induced by some zany Saturday Night Live, Mad TV space drug—provided by Abbie Hoffman...But upon closer inspection, you find that your eyes or mind had not been affected by any space dust; for what you saw, it all was so. It all was very real! Go figure! But once again you had to return to that place that land where the sons of man cannot go. That place created by L'Ouverture, Ho Chi Minh, Castro. For they, the gray folk, had not yet reached the spiritual level of the zany sane folk with wooly hair—the mental state of the sanely folk who are ever in love with the life of all that dared to smile and sing the coming of "cataclysm"!

You have to believe in something that believes in you!

What do you mean?

Well, it seems that you think it is possible for you to go this life believing in nothing that is; yet tasting the insanity of knowing that which you believe in is dead. So, if it is dead, why do you believe in it?

That has to be some nonsense. I mean, could you really believe in something that is alive, yet dead, and come away feeling that what you believe in believes in you? I had to look at this question at some point in my life, and I do not believe that it makes much difference what I believe, then or now!

If you believe that then you believe in nothing. You talk of god and the saints of never can never, and now you bring this absurd notion of nonbelief to my home of spaced out order and anti-government sentiment, yet you believe not in any of these things. Nigga, you gone crazy!

I thought that we could have a dialogue, wherein neither one of us would have to be reminded of the self-hate that consumes us both. But I guess I was wrong.

VI

The Cat from Honduras

There was this cat from Honduras who could scarcely speak a word of English; he was the first cat that I met who was a Latino of Afrikan descent. I never looked at him as being any different from me, yet the

A DISJOINTED SEARCH FOR THE WILL TO LIVE | 42

other cats from where I was from, from this alien country, used to treat him as if he was an alien. I couldn't quite understand this behavior, but I didn't view him as being alien; as being different or separate from my identification as a "black boy." I understood that he was a black boy, like me, forced to dwell in an alien environment meant only to deform and misshape our evolution, our unfolding as human beings of Afrikan descent—just like our fathers before us. That alien environment being a State Reformatory for boys, an alien condition, an abnormal ambiance designed to make those of our kind alien to ourselves, to each other, and, most importantly, to those in our community.

During our stay in this state-run twilight zone, full of expendable human lives, black life, our lives, we refused the training for role as slaves—the permanent property of the State, society, and the future boom material for wall street's industrial index. The programs run by adult, so-called counselors, who bought and used drugs from us in the streets, weren't programs that we dared take part in, for we did not wish to become as they were: Broken Black men and women bent on living the lie of being normal in a society just equally bent on destroying the minds and lives, hopes and dreams of our own kind. That we were all alien for the hue in our skin didn't escape my consciousness. Yet this awareness of this state of oppression and exploitation mattered not for I had no way, no medium, through which I could develop and articulate this awareness of the lie of my kind's right to life— as articulated by the democratic nation-state called amerikkka the great. In short, no one really gave a fuck about the suffering of the ghetto child; they would just have us sing and rap about it, however, we better not do any active thing to change that condition. This I learned through my interaction with a cat from Honduras.

This cat was beautiful. I mean he would be putting me down with the fucked up conditions in his homeland; how the amerikkkans who came there were causing all the killing there, and be serious about sharing his experience with me. It didn't matter that we didn't know each other, to him the fact that I gave him the regard of respect, he in turn showed me the same regard in return. Though it was hard for me to follow him at first, as we communicated more I became in tune with his brand of english—it became our manner of communication, and the staff and the other cats in our unit could never figure out what it was we were talking about. We shared so much of our time together. I would tell him of stories about the shit I done seen go down in my community and he didn't believe me. He thought that we had it good in this country—he always talked of how the black folk down there in his country admired us, and tried to be like us black folk up here in amerikkka. The more we hung out with each other the more he came to see the fucked up way we had to exist in this so-called land of plenty and equality. He fast learned, through first hand experience, how those of my kind were treated by both black and whites alike, who represented the interest of the state and big business; he came to see on a certain level the hopelessness here that mirrored, in a lot of ways, the suffering back in his birth land.

The people on the staff, the so-called professional youth counselors, treated Rico like he was some sort of retard; they would use signing with their hands to attempt to communicate with him—he and I would later laugh at their ignorance, but I knew that this shit was belittling to this cat's self-image as a human being of Afrikan descent. A couple of times in our dorm area—the area in which we slept—I found him crying. This shit made me mad as hell. I understood his pain, because the fact is that I was treated the same way in school. Though I was born in this land and knew the master's english, I was treated like I was an alien, a retard, by the teachers, counselors, and people in general. When I was learning my ABCs, I recall very vividly being punished for not being able to get them as fast as my white counterparts; I was placed in a corner and told that I was, in so many words, stu-

pid. I told Rico this, and he said, "Damn, amigo, that some fucked up shit," in his best imitation of me. We were both born on the day after the fourth of July, and we were both 15 years old in the year of our lord 1987.

Though neither one of us could understand the hatred that we amerikkkan black boys displayed toward each other, we still attempted to keep the KKKer boys in check. We both understood that they hated the very ground each black boy walked on, so we made it our business to make their stay in that place very uncomfortable. This task was hard because we often had to go to war with our own kind over some bullshit. There was this one time when we both had to take on these cats from Park Heights. These were some troublesome young niggas, who were bent on taking Rico's shower shoes—though they used a poolgame as a pretense to open the way for the confrontation. They thought Rico weak and me crazy—their first and last mistakes, which gave us the ups. The damn fools ain't know him or me; if we had guns they would have died. The head cat called Rico a spic. Rico said nothing—he just smiled. I being one who didn't like name calling, or any of that talking shit, just sucker-punched the cat closest to me in his mouth with an overhand right, and the shit was on. We both knew that we would get our asses kicked, so we went straight hard, all out, fighting like our lives were on the line—which they were. A code red was called by Ms. White, the supervisor on at the time, and security was on the scene in a matter of minutes. They jacked us all up, taking us off to be placed on the isolation unit. We all dreaded having to go there, however, when it was time to represent we did just that, without second or third thought. We all stayed on lock down for about a week; they let us off, and them Park Heights cats thought Rico and me crazy, so they let us be.

Being that all we did most of the time was play cards, pool, and look forward to smoke break time, we all looked forward to the day we would be getting released from this farce of a place called "Training School." Rico had no family or home to speak of in this country. But he often would wonder out loud, "What is it that you going to do once you free?" I told him that I would first get some ass, get high, and go try to find some way to make money. There was no plans of going back to school—school wasn't even a thought in my mind, a part of my plan. He was under the misguided notion that if one was to educate one's self that all would be well. I had no such illusion. I told him that neither did the state, this is why they didn't give a fuck if we went to school while we were in this place of reform. We both laughed, and he said that he understood that reality. But I had no idea at that time that being in prison at 16, becoming state and private owned stock, was that part of the system's plan that I had no idea existed.

One day this redhaired, redeyed, palefaced kkker cat was giving a new kid a hard time—the kid was from around my block, and I couldn't let that fool mistreat him. Rico asked me what I wanted to do. I thought about it as we rode the bus to the chow hall for lunch. As we were going through the chowline, the redeyed cat got in line directly behind me, and my decision was made as I turned around and knocked his clown ass cold out. After seeing that my work was good and done, I proceeded to go through the chowline getting my hamburger, fries, greens, apple, and orange juice. Took my seat next to Rico and we ate our last meal together in peace, without saying a word. The pigs responded to the code red, they demanded that I get up against the wall, I refused. They attempted to manhandle me, Rico cracked the head pig over the head with his chair; I, in turn, shared my lunch with the entire goon squad. We did our dance of dominance and submission for at least 15 minutes, when finally reinforcement arrived and we were beaten down, without mercy or consideration, as if we were men—and we were since before we were born treated as such.

A week into our bid on isolation, without showers, the INS came and took Rico down south and finally home. I never heard from him again. Rico taught me of the suffering that all those who was brought to these shores in chains, traded and sold, whipped and kicked, displaced and scattered, denied and miseducated, twisted and bent, had to endure the hurtful ways of a colorless world order, in all of the amerikkkas—be we speaking master's english or spanish: "Off to jail you go, black-boy!" sings the reality of real life in the amerikkkas for those brought and sold to the amerikkkas.

VII

"Good morning," I have lost the social ability, a born right, to greet you, the morning rays of sunshine, the autumn breeze that carries the scent of the rain that fell the night before, the life-giving kisses of a warrior-queen with very soft lips. The freedom to greet each morning with "good morning" under normal conditions has been ripped from me—I who have developed my natural disposition to outwardly express my love for the beauty to be had from life: sweet, hot kisses, morning jogs through the park, conversations with the fellow next door, about the weather, while stretching after my run. This sad reality, for me, is not one that I have chosen, but one that I have been compelled to accept…in a place far from being my home.

"Good morning to existence in hell," is how I have been greeting each of the mornings of the past nine years I have spent in this dehumanized design called prison—many nights have been sleepless ones, whereby the morning finds me red-eyed, tired and determined not to be counted among the broken, the dehumanized victims. Though the majority of the time I awake feeling like I have died and gone to a place worse than hell, I still awake with the greeting of "good morning" on my lips. I guess this is just one of those habits folk in extremely repressive and crisis situations form as some means of creating an absurd routine that reflects the absurdity of their existence: no singing robins, no all-consuming hugs, no intense kisses, no "honey I love you" smiles, no eye-opening, mouth-watering smells of breakfast cooking in a kitchen peopled by those who mutually wish to be in your company, of their own free will. I still have yet to grow used to the dark and dingy gloom that roams throughout my mind, and the cage in which I dwell, when I awaken. "Good morning, existence in hell," has come to signal to me the fact that I have yet another day to spend in hell. I got to get up—this tedious process takes a while.

After having laid down in the bed for an extra five or ten minutes, 'cause generally I don't have no place to go, I can generally take my time to get out of my coffin marked "bunk" at a snail's pace. Sometimes I brush my teeth and wash my face, while other times I don't even bother (I like to use close-up as opposed to colgate, it has something to do with animal abuse experiments or it could be exploitation of child labor by big corporate interests—so colgate ain't to be used...but close-up is made by the same company, I guess I got to start using soap to clean my breath and teeth...Oh well, such is the sacrifices needed to be made by a true revolutionary). I do more than I don't when I think about it, because my breath do be smelling foul and the taste in my mouth be too close to that of dog dung, which I in turn use to keep the punk police and simpleton breed of inmates out of my face, my way, my sight—I often smile to myself because of my use of this foul-smelling tactic; though rarely do I employ it, I come to find its use to be very effective...Even if I do or don't wash my face or brush my teeth, I will most definitely take a piss and/or shit—lighting a homemade air freshener, made of toilet paper and scented oil, which you light with a match when ready to use...With my scented toilet paper ablaze, as I sit upon the white porcelain dung and piss eater, I read from Comrade George's *Soledad Brother*—which is my morning

A DISJOINTED SEARCH FOR THE WILL TO LIVE

T'ai Chi—with Tupac's creative genius flowing throughout the cage...With a jailhouse blunt burning between my lips, opening my mind's eye, while still on the white porcelain dung and piss eater, I am turning over in my mind what actually it is I will be doing that day.

The activity I plan for any given day is always dealing with tasks of my individual character growth and development, resolving the internal contradictions that cause my kind so much personal pain, with the application of tenets handed down by those who went before; tenets that inform me of what it is I need to do to help in the creation of the new reality, a New Afrikan world-view that embraces and affirms the value and worth of all Afrikan life. I ain't with none of the slavish reactionary and non-thinking activity—Basketball, Bullshittin', Backbiting, and more Basketball—that is the norm of this dehumanized design called prison. Our keepers keep the basketball, weights, and drugs flowing, while keeping the needed vocational and educational needs of the captives inadequate or nonexistent...Reading Bakunin and Berkman on the political point; studying Kom'boa Ervin and Kropotkin, and dialoguing with Comrade Fanon and Freire, or just kicking back, reflecting on the fucked up state of the world or remembering that "What has been imagined need not be forgotten," and with these concepts and visions playing throughout my essence, I move out over the earth, to and fro, defeating the foes of New Afrika with great ease and grace—with both George and Jon Jackson at my side. It is this exercise that I enjoy doing the most because it is where my New Afrikan ideals come into play—my chance to dialogue with a whole host of revolutionaries of various ideological tendencies, though the majority of these comrades have what is the sum total of an Afrikan-centered world view, I nonetheless still enjoy kicking it with so-called communist thinkers. What the hell!

At these times in the morning hours, just before breakfast, I turn over in my mind the reality that surrounds me, the things I must do to remain sane, and the future that I hold with me—the courage and the ability to create a new reality. I say to myself: I, as an individual, must be free of this concentration camp, prison, that has held my body in chains—behind an inhuman wall of insanity, lies, and amerikkan chattel laws, since I was but a confused and suffering lad of sixteen, and being today a dashing young man of twenty-six, razing this hell is my number one goal. Breaking free of the mind-numbing stupidity which is inherent in the very idea of such places as prisons, I strive to break free into freedom. Family life, walks through the park, not fearing to live and to enjoy life! Not having to deal with the sickness and insanity of these so-called brothers and sisters wearing the uniforms of the department of incorrection.

From this cage, which is smaller than the average monkey's or gorilla's cage in a zoo, I wage war with the ruling families' forces of reaction—the police, national guard, us marines, etc.—in my attempts to defend the mass commune. New Afrikan liberation struggles be in full swing, from a cage in a gulag marked "grave", from the mind of a captive/combatant who ain't supposed to be capable of saying "Muthafuck Fascism, Capitalism, and Imperialism, the children of European supremacy." But I do! So, in essence, let's raze European hegemony…And in the next moment, it is time for breakfast, it is about 5:00 AM—the sun hasn't come up yet.

To breakfast and back, feeling as if I hadn't ate a thing, cursing all the pigs to hell, in my mind, as I pass them by on the walk from the chow hall back to the cage. I quickly forget about my hunger when I begin to think of the struggle to regain my liberty and the case law I sent out for last month—wondering about why it is taking those library people so long to get it to me. I am incessantly thinking about and working towards regaining my stolen freedom. My fellow captives tell me that

I should loosen up a little, that I should slow my roll, that I should take a chill pill before I have a stroke or something. And I tell them that they should mind their mothafuckin' business and not mine, that I am an innocent man, and the victim of euroamerikkkan supremacist injustice and its prison industrial complex—as they themselves are, but are too cowardly or indoctrinated to know or care. That because they have been compelled through a life of aimless existence, deferred dreams and ambitions, they have grown adjusted to the status of slave, captive, a caste of untouchables...Their contentment with being in this concentration camp has nothing to do with me—I refuse to ever accept this situation of captivity. And they still don't understand why I am the way that I am...the innocent man.

VIII

Alpine was a slave who was maced in the face and thrown down a flight of stairs simply for saying no to repression. A gray haired old nigga who knew my dead dad well was maced and thrown down a flight of stairs with fettered hands and bloody mouth, landing head first, simply because he dared be brave heart and TRU. Rattling the cage of repression with the love lust of sanity and a wild and free spirit of justice, he prayed to his humanity for the assistance that was not at hand from his fellow captives; slaves who were all around as the devil's helpers kicked his ass without fear of any sort of interference or rebellion of major depth. All the slaves walked away with heads bowed and code of honor between their hind legs. In this house of confusion, the rattling of cages is rewarded with bowed heads, whispered courage, and openly expressed hatred for he who dare do a bit of rattling.

Flowing through the mind of this rebellious human being, who dared think himself to be human, flowed the images of life as he received the slave's treatment with fire still in his belly:

House of confusion, full of delusions, a place where mace is sprayed in the face of indignant slaves refusing to go to the grave of sublime submission, bent minds, broken spirits. Rattling the cage of repression, grabbing at the yoke of exploitation, attempting to curtail its stinging bite of flesh, this unbroken spirit reaches forth to pull from the hands of the evildoer the power of life and death...genocide for economic status and a blood-stained law and order.

All in the church cursing the very existence of their own wretched lives...Praising their dead lord, who stood on the banks of the james river in 1712, informing his fellow lords of the fool-proof plan of breaking horses: the kind with two legs, dark skin, and Sphinx-building blood flowing through their eternal, ageless minds—which is possessed by lord lynch, the amerikkkas, europe, and asia, from then to now.

IX

Viewing Heaven from Hell

There is a window in the building, inside the prison, that separates me from the living, and acts as a beautiful vista into the life, the world, of which I am denied. Through this window I have a view of the carefree movements and activity of that day unfold before my longing eyes— done through the window of the prison that holds me; watching a honeybee alight upon a dandelion full of her needed honeymaking sustenance. A wonderful interaction between a wild cat and her litter of six kittens progressing before my eyes, unhindered by the foulness of this blighted concentration camp that now inhibits my ability to be one in free and natural activity with them...

Just watching these natural activities unfold touches and fills every fiber of my soul with pure joy, and a wee bit of envy. The cat and her litter of six kittens, which are all pink, the honey bee alighting on the dandelion, and all the natural activities that unfold, through this caged in window, are not missed by me. Despite the evil of the reality created by man—a reality that is presently threatening to push out of existence the beauty of the natural life that I now attempt to share—I can see beyond the ugliness that he has built in the name of progress and civilization, "Law and Order." I can see through the alienating walls of his skyscrapers, malls, and extravagant technological advancements, see through the separation of humanity from nature and its self—I do understand the fundamental baseness of his unnatural world-view.

So, as I continue to gaze on the love of life, in this cruel and unusual manner, my undying and ever-present friends(longing to feel my gentle touch fall upon them), begin to call for my attention, and implore me to break free from the zoo which restricts gaze and touch from fully reaching them. They whisper my name, and the breeze brings it to me. Because I cannot hear this call of my friends—for the thickness of the repressive glass blocks the call from reaching my ears—a fallen branch or some fallen leaves are sent, carried by the wind to strike that which prevents their message of love and resistance from reaching my ears. I hear this, raising my head with a grin, I mentally greet them, and quickly apologize for not having the strength to break the chains that keep me from the embrace of life's grace.

With my full and undivided attention now given to them, my friends, *who are beyond the repressive confines of the walls, the bars, and the razor wire-laced fences, give me a wide natural smile, a smile full of nature's life force—they understand! These living creators, uncontaminated by the lifelessness that surrounds and confounds me, are the natural inhabitants of this island world where the window that I view and commune with them is at. They surround that which surrounds me on all sides; that which seeks to contaminate and thus destroy my humanity, my sanity, my spirit.*

They call to me! They inspire me! They give to me that which this hell tries every second of the day to deny me! Love, life, light, and every thing that gives purpose and meaning to all living creatures! To me the creatures of nature whisper: "That which has been imagined need not be forgotten! That which is, that which seeks to control and dominate us, life, will one day be put back in its place, made to leave, we who seek to remain connected to that which bonds all living things together, alone!...Just continue to be yourself: Brave and True to the liberation of New Afrika and humanity!"

When back in the cage, I quickly began to write that which you all now read: The Odyssey of a New Afrikan Man-Child! When the gates of resistance fly open the dragon will surely come forward transformed, resurrected like the Phoenix soaring on high, with all of its friends that now assist me. "Forward, onward to victory!" they will sing. As they bring the reawakened example of that which gives meaning and purpose to all human life: truth, love, justice, equality, food, clothing, shelter, and the right to life and peaceful assembly for all.

"Alive and kickin'!" I be full of aliveness and New Afrikan flames of humanity in spite of all the denaturalized and despirited baseness that surrounds me.

X

Remembering Dee

There once was a prostitute named Dee, who I went to see regularly. When but 14, I had my first full-fledged sexual experience with this Black woman who had to turn tricks to make ends meet. She had a pimp, with a limp and an unfriendly grin, who owned a fine Caddie, expensive gold chains and bracelets, silk and leather suits—all which was bought and paid for with Dee's money. It was in this car (by rights Dee's car) that we did our business—in an alley, in an uncharming city, in its downtown business district where movers and shakers of the underground economy came above ground to conduct their business. The criminals in business suits show their (masked with smiles) faces during the day, while victims of the parasitic economic arrangement, that gives life to the criminals in business suits, come out at night with unmasked smiles of scares, tears, and a desire to survive the lived paradigm of social Darwinism—the rat race.

One moonless midnight, I sensed a change in Dee's generally sunny disposition. She seemed to be a thousand miles away in her mind, off to a place that only she could know. After taking care of our business interaction, while I was pulling on my tennis shoes, she turned her blackened eyes onto me, and for the first time I realized, because the starless sky had prevented me, that her pimp had beaten her up—I knew it was him for her brown eyes told me as much.

With a rage and determination I had not up until that time witnessed written all over her face, she says to me: "Tony, that is the last time that nigga is going to beat me...I mean that shit!" with tears streaming down her cheeks. "He's taking all my money, I can't even feed my kids, pay the rent, or get my hair and nails done! I have to do something." Having said this to me, Dee lapsed into a coke-induced daze—before we began takin' care of business we did a few lines of cocaine. Coke which I provided; coke which I sold as an up and coming ghetto star—so I thought and believed in my own battered child's mind.

Not knowing what to say I asked her what does she want me to do? Being young, a child with a gun, I did not think to consider the consequences of my involvement. It took her a moment or so to respond to my sincere but very naïve inquiry. Thoughts of bravado, of being the dark knight in shining armor, on the shores of Angola, defending the honor of my Queen, as I awaited her response, ran through my illicit mind—I smiled. Dee finally answered, but she didn't answer my question: "I have to get away from this cold-hearted nigga! If he thinks he is gonna take care of his habit off of me, he has to be crazy…I shouldn't have never gotten involved with that asshole…I am leaving that bastard—fuck him!"

Feeling as if she was ignoring me, I repeated my inquiry that was in fact a request: "What do you want me to do, Dee?" She smiled at me, kissed me on my cheek and said that our business transaction was on her; that I could keep my money; that I was very sweet. I took my leave, thanking her, wishing her well, already missing her smile—knowing that I would probably never see her again.

So young and naïve, yet so old and wise, was I. Though I never laid eyes on Dee's billion dollar smile or her bomb body again, it wasn't these things that made her special to me. It was her spirit and daring that compelled me to see my own self, my own ability to rebel against that which sought to enslave me. As she did with her pimp, I too did with the world—I questioned, I dared to see myself as an actor, as a shaper of my own tomorrows. I saw myself as a human being.

XI

No Love

"What the fuck you mean you ain't got no money, nigga? You better dig in your dip and kick out that loot you got stashed there!"

"Look man, I ain't got shit! You done already checked my pockets...What you want me to do? If I ain't got no money, I ain't got none."

With the burning desire that comes with having the unsatisfied hunger of the generation made victim of a war that their elders failed to teach them about, the unfolding of this all too familiar urban event did not go unnoticed by those who went before these two ghetto youth—the victims: the robber and the robbed.

"Nigga, just take off all your shit, now!" Motioning with the police issue .38, the robber indicated to his victim what he meant for him to take off—his clothes. "And nigga, I mean your underwear too."

"Why the fuck you robbing me, man? I'm just like you—I ain't got shit! I'm a nigga struggling to survive just like you, but I ain't into robbing folk that ain't got shit; folk who are being fucked around the same as me." With his eyes on the gun of his assailant, his focus locked on the black abyss that was the hole in the barrel, the victim gives his words full of a truth alien to the robber. A robber who is himself the victim of crack addiction—his escape from the reality conveyed to him by his fellow sufferer.

Having his victim remove all of his clothing, underwear included, the robber looked on the pile of clothing, suddenly completely hating himself, his life, and the big mouth nigga who stood before him. He thought of Robin, his woman and crack smoking partner, and her sadness of having him return home without any money. Having been out all night and most of the morning, the robber was full of the feeling of being denied something. Not really understanding why the words of the man who stood before him bothered him; why his words stirred within him feelings of humiliation and depravation that were much akin to the experience of he himself being robbed of something. The fact that his body and mind were screaming for a fix, a hit from the pipe, was having no effect on him, the robber's spirit was moving him to a place beyond the base desire that was now causing his body to shake and sweat, and his mind to threaten to spill completely over to insanity. He started to cry.

His victim stood before him without a stitch of clothing on his back, with the cool morning air sending chills up his spine, and with the shame of his nudity having fixated itself at the forefront of his mind, he watched as the robber stood there before him, with his eyes fixed on the heavens, tears rolling down his brown face, and smiling. The victim moved to retrieve his clothing, when without warning the robber stirred from his trance. Fixing his eyes on his victim, the robber posed a very profound question:

"Why—why do I hate me?"

Dumbfounded, the victim simply replied: "Because we haven't been given no reason to love us."

PART THREE

I

He remembers and writes; writes and remembers. He hopes and dreams; dreams and hopes. Yet in his world, in every corner, resides the all-illuminating beautified death of she with the name of a virgin. He lives in a hole that has been raised to raze the illuminating power of his life force; however, he thought such a power to be dead and gone—never to return to his mind full of calm seas and clear night-time sky. With the longing of a slave to be free, he ate rice and fish. With a can of pepsi to wash down the gritty slime of a time spent away from home, he watched a television that blinded all who viewed it with a closed mind; a mind blind to the evil that lurked and oozed from behind the one-eyed disseminator of hate and disgrace.

Making no sense out of the aims of the people he called his own, he decided to ignore their trained dog-like behavior. Keeping their eyes on a prize that had no corresponding bearing on the horrible trials and hard times that their sons and daughters daily confronted 'til death or worse: a life time in a place raised to raze their entire lives. From schools that hurt the creativity of their natural gifts to create and build those things that compliment the reality of humanity's connection to the earth, the entire universe, they move out to deal a dream that was dreamt by those who live in heaven on earth at the expense of their Black life. He tried to make sense out of their hatred for him, the cold-hearted disdain for him, his kind, his lot. I mean, after all, these were supposed to be his people, his kin. His kin, who chased after bones and crumbs thrown down by Peter, Paul, and Mary, seemed to openly be in love with that which he fought so hard to be rid of within himself...

He is told he is now amerikkkan, but he don't want to accept this lie; he would rather fight to regain and build that which had been razed by those who now say he is free. The walk through amerikkka, his life in this society has informed him that Mary will not be happy until this world is no more, and Mars becomes the home planet of those who build bombs that kill human flesh yet save buildings made of concrete and steel. With Reaganomics came a form of poverty that left the ghetto victims foolishly believing themselves the cause of their lot. They somehow forgot that the full reality of responsibility minus self-determination equals the black amerikkkan colony. With meaningless promises, we spent the 1980s helping in the destruction of the minds of our own children. Our hero is the product of the decade full of Iran-Contra, Kneegrow Jesse running for the pale house, the crack attack, bloods and crips, CIA sponsored drug importation, selling and genocide, project push, headstart and unnumbered other governmental programs sponsored for the sole purpose of repressing the desire to be free within the Afrikan child and replacing it with the illusion of inclusion in a society that cannot function without the ghetto child as social, economic, political, and cultural fodder.

She attempted to make him submit to the role of fodder, of human being of unvalue. However, he struggled to make something of himself. He struggled to find answers to the questions that burned in his heart. He always struggled with the weakness, the desire to accept his role, to simply submit. But something deeper within him refused outright to ever allow him to be comfortable with himself if he did such a thing. So assimilating to the ways of the dominant culture was out, yet and still, he had to wrestle with the bitch, the product of his socialization, the blight of all human life. He was the rejected, yet he somehow retained within himself the hope and longing to be accepted and embraced by those who rejected him outright; those who refused to give unto him the human consideration and respect one human gives to the next. This was a collective search for meaning, a collective struggle to come to terms with the true nature of the Afrikan twisted into the image of the invader—the destroyer of human holistic societies.

He remembers and writes; writes and remembers! He hopes and dreams; dreams and hopes from a cell, in a place constructed to impose and fulfill his role as fodder, as a human of nonvalue. He sits and waits for the coming of the dragon, the coming of the gods and saints from the innerworld of Afrikan unfolding, hope and undying resistance. Writing about a reality denied and ignored by the victims of it, he refused to kill himself in an act of refusing to continue living as fodder in a world not created by his ancestors for him and his. He put away the whip of self-doubt, self-murder, and self-castration, and brought forth the names of his 20th century greatest men and women—he drew strength from the bloodshed, the spirit of resistance left to him and his generation. He dismissed the confused rage of the Thug Nigga in him, he laughed at the backwardness of co-opted hip hop culture, he understood that Black folk's suffering wasn't for sale; that rappers, designers, producers, and followers of this hip hop bastard had to be seen for the genocidal promoters that they had willingly become—killers of resistance culture for the capitalist motivation of the amerikkkan dream.

It is Black life, Afrikan life, that he had come to value above all else. He had to learn to love himself as an Afrikan, a human being of a proud past to be embraced and never rejected; a history to be praised and exalted beyond the stars. He felt the unity of life that was nearly destroyed by the lies of his acceptance into a culture that refused to respect that which it treated as their property; he felt the love of himself rocket above the morbid constraints of his status as fodder. He negated and pissed on the european's way of ife, sense of morality, justice, and peace.

A DISJOINTED SEARCH FOR THE WILL TO LIVE

He thought of Fannie Lou Hamer, and kissed the thought of a black woman that he wished to Jah he could have met. He wrote about the fire within himself, the fire that reminded him of his daring attempt to simply "be":

Into the fire within I dare roam;
Into the unknown fire within I dare
brave to go, not fearing the tolling
of death's bells.

Into the fire within I dance;
Into the unknown fire within I go,
trusting to find my home away from
home.

Enticed by the fire within, calmly walking into the marrow of my soul, with the power of clairvoyance, I follow the rose-colored trail of tears into the fire of the unknown. Looking for home, not a house of brick or wood, but a house free of razor wire-laced fences, broken bottles, empty refrigerators, and malnourished stomachs filled with carry-out food. A home wherein roams love laced with joy and sorrow, smiles and frowns that expressed the willingness of all those that dwell therein to share the beauty and ugliness of life's realities, is the home within the fire that I seek.

The fire unknown bellows forth the ever-present cries and expired lamenting of all the slain hopes of those who went before, in this war, in this battle between the lost children of Eden and the debased but exalted sons of Cain. Through the fire I pilot winged-horse-drawn chariots of gold full of resistance fighters, money haters, and tamed insanity; looking to find our way home, safely away from cowardice and fear. Talking of sure-fire and fulfilled promises as we go along through the corridors of our own personal hells—in an attempt to understand our collective hell, hurt, alienation, and foe.

Consuming the untold stories of old, I shout out in an ancient tongue, declaring my undying loyalty to those undying spirits I have met in the fire unknown. Springing forth in the forgotten dance of yesterday's joy to all and peace on earth among the true hue-mens, I roll on earth's clay and mud, stand, gyrate my hips and spin myself in a fevered war-like circular movement that invokes the pious chants of my kind: Freedom 'til free! Slavery refused 'til free!

When flowers grow on the shores of our vision of a hue-man world, free of pale death, made so by and for the loved deferred children of the Amerikas, Afrika, Asia, Australia, and all the places where love once lived before the release of the pale horse rider of pestilence came forth bearing gifts of twisted material progress, talking machines, and non-feeling gods of death.

Coming forth from the fire within, the fire unknown, spring the singing, chanting, the roar of the children of the ghetto, of the reservation, of tin and cardboard tenements, of the children of yesterday, today, and tomorrow:

INTO THE FIRE WITHIN WE MUST ROAM;
INTO THE FIRE WITHIN WE MUST GO!
INTO THE FIRE WITHIN WE MUST DANCE,
SING AND FIGHT! INTO THE WITHIN WE MUST
GO: CLAIMING AND CALLING THE FIRE WITHIN
US OUR HOME 'TIL WE ARE ALL
FREE!

II

Dear X,

Just was setting here thinking of the fact that I haven't been socially in touch with myself for some time. Coming to the conclusion that this is the result of having to deal with so many backward and condensed personalities, I have had to acknowledge that I am now partially a cynic of some sort; a cynic in the context of not believing in the unselfish and authentic relations that could develop between two complete social strangers. Though this is a reaction that has been going on within me on an unconscious level, it has only been our recent interaction that has helped me come to see this development within myself. I think I have somehow allowed myself to deal with the dominant culture's definitions, to use them as if my own, as if they were the correct precepts to follow in the very process of communication. From the superficial to the in-depth layers of human interaction, I have lost touch in many ways.

No doubt it is hard not to want to feel the very human need to connect with someone of the same mind; but for me it has caused me many setbacks and heartaches. The setbacks have come as the result of me misplacing the glory with the shame: getting my priorities and focus for regaining my freedom mixed up with needing to have a connection with someone unconnected with my present situation. But the reality of my needs is tied into the fact that I needed to be connected to folk, people, who would support me in my fight. My emotional needs had to be placed on the back burner. Being that I had to come up in such an abnormal design of white death, I have had to attempt to grow and develop my humanity in spite of the obvious dehumanizing pressures. In such an attempt I have had to come to terms with a great many of my shortcomings.

By their very nature, prisons are designed to destroy the human being's ability to function socially with other human beings, i.e. family, friends, wayfarers and supporters. But above all else it is most effective in the process of alienation of the captive human being from him/herself. At the age of sixteen, I was shoved into this situation by a system that had no intention of having me survive this dehumanizing design. Educationally, when I entered this penal colony, I was reading and writing on a third grade level, and my mathematics abilities were appalling. My psychological and emotional abilities were on a level that reflected the arrested development of the environment out of which I came. I was born and raised in the city of Baltimore, MD, at a time when most of my kind were living under the illusion of "being free amerikkkans." In spite of the blatant fact that there was an obvious difference in the manner through which the wealth and privileges, power and security, were distributed within the larger socioeconomic and political arrangement. Under the illusion of equality and civil rights, the reality of human rights and the right of our kind, as an oppressed colony of the empire, self-determination was down-played and in the majority of cases, these things were simply ignored. Being completely unaware of the historical relations, the historical continuation of the slave/master relationship, between my kind and the settler class and his running dog lackey negroes, I moved throughout my time in that society totally unconnected to myself and the interests of my community. So, by the above brief and technical account of my upbringing, I shouldn't be of the presence of mind that I now exhibit. But I am!

Make no mistake about it, I do have purpose, direction, and identity. However, today, right here and now, I am taking the time out to share my past with you. It has never been an easy task for me to recount the typical tragedy that is the life of those of my kind. I think because the fact that the reality that the lot of the average New Afrikan, in this settler nation, is so common, that even those of us who suffer the bite of this unjust order tend to not fully appreciate the harm that is daily carried out against our humanity, our existence, our value as a people. I am constantly made to feel as if the world-view that I have is of no value; that I am supposed to simply go along with the agenda of the very system that seeks to push me out of this existence. I, of course, rebel against such thoughts that are generally pushed into my consciousness by the very people who suffer from this insanity called west ern civilization, i.e. through the music, literature, newspapers, TV, and the day to day interactions with the world via my present status as captive, criminal, slave.

Believe me, I do understand that we are in a very fucked up situation—a situation that is designed to prevent those of our inclinations from coming together. There are many barriers that have been placed in front of our kind; barriers that keep us divided and scattered the world over. But I refuse to allow such a condition to stifle me, and I hope that you are (still) of the same mind on this point. The bottom line of all that I have written above is this: Please, do not run from that which is naturally occurring; resist the enemy's powers to destroy the life yet born, newly born—the life that is to be found in the revolutionary act of simply caring for someone, daring to understand someone, who cares and dares to authentically and unselfishly do the same with you. Feel me! Now let us grow into this friendship with such an acceptance and understanding of the above stated purpose, intentions, and causes which we both believe in! Let us be Brave Heart and TRU friends.

Here I would like to share some things about myself with you...For the majority of my adult life, throughout the entire course of my growth and development as a revolutionary, I had been full of a pride and dignity that had caused me to become reactionary in a lot of ways. In ways such as my refusal to accept assistance from those with a vested interest in this system. Now, this sort of behavior flew in the face of the reality of my situation, and contradicted my efforts to regain my stolen liberty—negated my needs for assistance. I had allowed my need to assert my consciousness of the true nature of this unjust order to override the reality that I need to be liberated first—as it is obvious that I would be more effective in this struggle with my freedom of movement unfettered by these bars, walls, gun towers, and razor wire. At that phase of my growth and development, I had not yet developed the mental and intellectual sophistication of the guerrilla. In this war of attrition, as a guerrilla in the undeclared people's army, I am just learning the strategic and tactical skills necessary for me to become conscious of the psychological and emotional methods of attrition employed by the system, in its efforts to wear down and destroy the consciousness of those of my kind, who have against all odds developed an anti-capitalist inclination. This pride and dignity of which I speak is necessary and develops, in time, out of one's continued struggle to free their humanity from the illusions of social and political justice in an unjust order. But I attempted to assert my consciousness only because I wasn't yet confident enough in my ability to be effective in my delivery of my consciousness through my efforts to assist in the shaping of the new reality. This sort of behavior has almost cost me my sanity, pride and dignity, my very life…Nothing has been easy about my evolution!

I came into the consciousness of my status as amerikkka's fodder when I was about 17 years old. This process began as I sat in a cell, completely naked, on the unit for the mentally ill convicts. I had yet to learn how to read and write on a functional level, but the intense and repressive humiliation that I suffered sitting in that cell compelled me to take my own destiny in hand. The human being unfortunate enough to be on this ward had to endure daily cell searches. The pigs said that this practice was done for our own protection, but the reality was that these very sick white men wanted to sexually and psychologically torture those who would not present resistance to their advances. For those of us who did resist, we were outright denied all three meals, walks and shower time, and ultimately beaten for being "bad niggers." How I made it through those months spent on that unit is an experience that I will not tell until I am out of this hell—the shit I had to endure there still causes me nightmares. They used to have group meetings every week in this room that had a variety of books and recreational equipment. During one such meeting, I had expropriated for myself a dictionary, a pencil, and a writing tablet. And for the next four months, for at least 12 hours out of each day, I grilled myself as I studied that dictionary from cover to cover. However, the first words that I learned came from this psychology college textbook I also procured from the group therapy room. Information and manipulation were the first two words that I learned. I recall very vividly that I had to write on the bare walls of the cell, because I had no paper, as I drilled myself on the spelling and meaning of those words. I remember having to sit on the floor, cross-legged, as I strained to read and comprehend words and concepts that I had never known existed. When I left that psych ward, I never looked back; and I have never, and will never, return to that state of unconsciousness that has given this system the ability to hold claim over my person up to this very day.

Take care! Keep your head up! Stay strong! And know that my thoughts are with you!

Sowed and reaped,
The man without a name.

III

How dare he speak
to those outside of
his hell in such
an intelligent tone,
in such an
insightful manner,
in such an unbecoming
style for the socially
dead nigger that he is!

This nigga is above himself,
he isn't supposed to be able
to question his master's
ways of mastering his slaves.

Especially not in such
a nonconformist,
anti-authoritarian,
Black-life affirming critique
of that which is supposed
to be above his intellectual
capabilities.

This nigga is the child
of that place where
niggas are not ever
supposed to rise above!
Mother Mary has seemed
to have failed with
this one.

This nigga seems
to have made it.

"Has he?"

"I doubt it!"

'Cause we know that watermelon,
chicken,
and dope
are his kind's favorite
excuse to forsake all
that they claim to stand for.

Chicken,
Watermelon,
and Dope
are what can be

bought with the money,
or just the promise
of a whitewoman,
that we can provide them.

Just give the nigga
some greenbacks
and all of his pain
and suffering will
miraculously disappear.

If he won't bite,
we'll just send one
 of his hungry brothers
or sisters to bite
him for us.

His bark means nothing;
his voice will not be
heard over the maddening din
of his backward people—
out to make a way out
of the whiteway;
paperchasing.

IV

I have the likenesses of George Jackson and Tupac Shakur tattooed forever, side by side, on my right forearm, on my gun hands. Until I'm dead and gone, these two Afrikan Warriors from two seemingly different paths, will ride with me—informing me to "Stay True." From "Thug Life" to "Revolutionary Life," these two brothers from two different generations, coming forth from the same womb of pain and suffering which is produced by the same negation: the absence of New Afrikan independence and self-determination; will forever remind us of the evil that men do—the evil that this european reality creates and maintains, promotes and imposes on those of us whose natural worldview presupposes the sacredness of all living things, the connection of every living thing to every other living thing, bound by the cords of life, death, and from death back to life again.

With George, I have blood in my eye, guerrilla warfare in my veins, and in my soul the will and determination to help build the new reality he lived and died for. From the burning flames of this hell I will rise with his name and memory burning bright in my heart and mind, and in my soul the suffering, the courage, the defeats, the victories and the love of all the generations of sufferers, resisters, and inspirers will reside. Coming forth by night, we will not, never, ever forget the death camps, the tortured trails through the interior of our native lands in chains, across the middle passage to the shores of this god-forsaken land, in pain and misery…And the death of a thousand cuts will not deter our advance to freedom this time.

With Tupac, I have opened fire, Ride or Die, on the enemies of New Afrikan liberation and self-determination, and in my heart I feel his pain, the pain of our generation; the pain of a lifetime of masked lies and open despise of our kind—from ourselves, produced by those who lie and despise us all. And I will forever be still down with the creative genius of this much misunderstood child of Afrika—with all of his contradictions, confusions, and illusions. And still I ain't got nothin' but love for him, my generation of sufferers, resisters, and inspirers…'cause I overstand the paleman's master plan…it won't work, can't work, 'cause we're riding, in spite of all the dying on our side of the battlefield of life and death.

With George and Tupac forever tattooed on my gun-slinging arm, as we ride for the freedom of our nation, the liberation of our children from the clutches of white supremacy, the vision of self-determination, independence, homes, food, and clothes for New Afrikans in Amerikkka will become that new reality our fore mothers and fathers sighed and cried, prayed and begged, fought and died for! The feds killed their bodies but they can never kill the spirit; for in us all it resides, so let us ride!

We are damned if we don't…and damned if we do!—so many of the naysayers and do-nothings would have us believe. But do we must! We must learn to do for our own, damned or not! The struggle for the continuation of our kind hangs on the rekindling of that spirit, creative genius, and collective love and commitment that made our forebears the bearers of civilization and humanity! Let us reclaim that which is ours by birth right; let us reclaim our history, our minds, our children…with George and 'Pac we must ride…or we will surely die. But worse, our very existence will be cursed by our unborn generations if we fail to do what must be done…if we are to survive ourselves, as a whole people, in mind, body, and spirit.

Forever tattooed on my heart and mind, forever George, Tupac, and I will ride on the enemies of our kind! There is no end to these lines full of collective love and rage; no end 'til all are free. So, let us ride for freedom and justice, for a new tomorrow, today!

PART FOUR

I

The tortured soul of a man struggling to become one who honors life's beauties. A misunderstood man, an abused man. With the many abuses of the earth, this man attempts to touch it all before it is all gone: the trees, the rolling hills, the red and gray sky, the rain-filled clouds. Probing his soul for the genius that had brought man out of darkness into the light of day; reaching back into his ancestral memory to retrieve the grandness of innocence lost, beauty squandered, love debased.

With an age-old aching in his heart, he screams out to the world his search of loss and confusion: the loss of light of humanity; the confusion of civilization with barbarism! How odd and sad he feels when he witnesses the uncaring lies, masked as truth, that are daily told by those who claim to represent the interests of the people, the security of the people, the moral character of the nation. They praise the living document that wasn't written to include those of us with hue, that is supposed to be the blueprint which the entire world is to bow down to in submission, "for the lord guided the hand of the forefathers of this nation to write such a moral and legal document." The oddness comes when he finds himself restricted, unable to say the truth and move the people to action, speaking through the wind that moves through the hair of a child at play.

Without the peace that comes with freedom, he watches the children of the earth move across the face of their Mother without a clue as to why they suffer so very much; children who don't know from where the truth is to be told. With the blood-soaked earth underfoot, they run a race that has no winners, a marathon that has no rules. Up the hill of the embattled crossroads of life, they exist only to make the super-rich more so; to help make the evil ones place their children in the chains of the New World Order. Eking out the living of a mole without a hole to call home, they blindly reach to the heavens upside down in a world where there is no up or down, right or wrong.

The tortured soul of a man, entombed in a world with many walls and bars where the sun and stars don't shine, in a world where love is a word often used but never heard. In such a world this tortured soul yells for the hell to freeze over, screams for the morrow to be brighter, shouts for the scouts from other worlds to detour around this mad one, bellows for the unborn not to leave the warmth and safety of their mother's womb…he shouts for all the lights to go out; for he hopes that once out, after a while, they will be turned back on and the beauty debased would have returned renewed, regenerated, reborn.

Entombed in gloom and doom, the tortured soul of a man rolls a cigarette, smiles, then softly cries, as the beast coldly yells: "LIGHTS OUT!"

II

He is at home with intellect, very much so, but he has no peace within his soul. He doesn't seem to be able to find solace in the fact that he has become more than a culturally constructed 'backward-21st century-Sambo ghetto-dwelling, slated-for-a-life-in-and-out-of-various-types-of-concentration-camps nigga.' Witnessing the daily murder of his humanity, he tries to cope, but cannot fail to take note of the deplorable state of his kind. For him, there is no ignoring the decline of Black love; there was no way that he could deny the reality of the terrible poverty of the soul, mind, and heart that now besieges his kinfolk. No compassion, hope, or desire to combat that which daily continues to negate the value and relevance of Afrikan life, black life. He tries to move through the endgame of his time in hell, a prison cell, as he watches the descent of his brothers in the painful acceptance of their chains, their existence in correctional institutions, mental wards, cardboard homes, and ghetto fame. Locked into the culture of the slave, calling it thug life, and missing out on the true necessity of creating a culture of resistance, as opposed to one of conformity to the status of amerikkkan fodder...He cannot turn his head from the war that rages all around him. The turning of the storm that engulfed him when he first heard the word nigger would not release him, and he refused to release himself. So he just sat back and awaited the coming of Marcus Garvey—looking to the eye of the storm.

Finding himself unable to watch the evening news—full of big city body counts of dead black life, forsaken life—he rolls over onto his side as he hears an approaching pig's keys rattle, as he counts the bodies of the cargo in the slaveship that doesn't move or float. One body among many, one mind that is being smothered by its own awareness of the reality of all that "is," with no illusions of ever becoming completely free—even after the chains were taken away from his body...However, he would rather be smothered by the truth than illusions, so he yells, "No more Dan Rathers, *60 Minutes, 20/20, Nightline,* Local News lies of 'It's a wonderful life' in the dark continent of amerikkka!" He demanded "More reality, laced with hope and a revolutionary romanticism that smells of shit-covered roses!"

III

Photographic Passion

In all the places for
a tale of an all
consuming passion
filled wonder
taking shape,
tenderly grabbing
a hold of a man's heart...
if one had an ideal place
where such a profound
human feeling was to be had,
it sure wouldn't be in a
concentration camp...

Yet, it has occurred for me,
to me,
in this most unlikely
and unideal place:
in a prison,
in a cell,
with insanity
and alienation
as the dominant features
making up the landscape
of twisted minds,
bent bodies,
and broken spirits...

the creation of a system
designed to twist,
bend,

and break its rejected,
despised,
oppressed,
and exploited human cargo,
is not the place for such
arousing
and inspiring feelings,
love thoughts
to be had;
for the unfulfilling
nature of its purpose
would leave one longing to live
and be dead
all at once,
in the same thought,
in the same vain breath.

You,
the Angel of my dreams,
came to me,
in spite of the
ugliness that
surrounds me.

In the form of a photograph
you came to me;
it was in the form
of a photograph that you,
that elusive
and fabled Angel
of all my sweet,
sensual,
tender dreams,
came to make yourself

A DISJOINTED SEARCH FOR THE WILL TO LIVE

known to me in this nightmare
filled reality.

In a photograph of a
woman simply sitting
in a crowded room,
I discovered you:
my very own cinderella.

With such aliveness did
my heart
and mind
respond to this
remitted
and
much anticipated
discovery
of romantic love.

As my deep felt elation subsided,
a degree or so,
the fact that I did not
know who this
Romantic and Revolutionary
looking woman was;
this woman who stood out
in a sea of other unknown faces;
who stood our because of
the magic that flowed from
the erotic positioning of
her voluptuous body,
the slight bend of her creamy
tanned neck,
the way her legs were carnally crossed..

Off in a corner
where she sat by herself,
not looking alone,
or looking as if she
were attempting to be antisocial...

Naw,
it had nothing to do
with such thing.

For me
it was simply
the inner knowing
that came along with
the first glance of her
which moved me to the point of...
almost falling in love
with a photograph.

However, before I lost all sense of space and time I regained my composure and decided that if I fell in love "why not fall in love with the real thing..."

IV

I love the music of Joan Baez and Joni Mitchell, James Taylor and Carol King, and I am New Afrikan. I am even down for hard stuff like Black Sabbath and Iron Maiden, Guns n Roses and Green Day, Pearl Jam, Radiohead, Ozzy, The Cure, and I am New Afrikan. Many of my comrades and friends do not seem to understand this phenomenon—a conscious New Afrikan man grooving to such tunes.

When confronted with the questions, "why you listen to whiteboy music," and "don't you think it's a contradiction?" I simply answer—to these brothers who seem to forget that they too possess like contradictions; some far deeper than my listening to "whiteboy music"—that "There isn't one New Afrikan born in Amerikkka who has not such contradictions, and for the majority of us, such contradictions go undetected. The greatest contradiction is created simply by the fact that we are an Afrikan people who have been socialized in a system/society dominated and controlled by a european people; we speak a european language, thus we think in european even when we are thinking Afrikan, for the end product of our thoughts will be translated into the english that we speak. To be clear on these facts doesn't mean that I am saying in any way that we cannot be Afrikan-centered in our world-view, but to attempt to deny the existential reality that for the majority of our lives, as an Afrikan people, we have been viewing the world through the eyes of the european—his world-view has been made ours.

"Have we forgotten the process of european cultural imperialism, the process that our open enemy has put us all through? He has made the world in his image and after his likeness, taken the ways of our forebears from us, indoctrinating us into an acceptance of his individualist and profane world-view. Each of you conscious men understand that we are just, in the twentieth century, regaining a true sense of our Afrikan selves. That which this european has taken from us will not be regained back overnight, especially not after over 400 years of history spent in an insanity called amerikkka, and then the history of our own individual experiences of being exposed to the deadly effects of the culture of death. We each have had (and if we haven't, we have to) to wage an internal struggle to disengage the full effect of our enemy's world-view, replacing it step by step, collectively, with an Afrikan-centered world-view. It will take time, but we will have to do it if we are ever going to win that which is ours by birthright: Independence and Self-determination. Feel me."

I sometimes have to give them a little history of what they wrongly call "whiteboy music." My brothers generally associate rock and roll, heavy metal, and punk with being creations of white folk. So, I refresh their memories to the screaming indignant guitar god Jimi Hendrix, and the fact that the european press themselves called the thunder tones he played "heavy metal"—this term was first used to describe Jimi's music. I go on to mention the fact that Chuck Berry, Little Richard, and Fats Domino were the true pioneers of Rock and Roll, but because of the music industry's white supremacist mentality, these brothers didn't receive their due. Then I give them the history of the blues, and the fact that rock and roll is nothing but the blues speeded up—and that the term rock and roll was a term first used by our ole folk down south in daily conversations to talk of the sex act, the nasty, knockin' boots, etc., long before rock and roll was called rock and roll. And punk rock, well, I don't usually get this far.

Oh well, the truth is that the majority of the time this doesn't fly with my brothers, but because they see the Afrikan in my actions and deeds, they walk away with at least a better understanding of the workings of the consciousness of this New Afrikan who listens to "white boy" music.

V

He thought of soapbox orators back in the days of zoot suits and conk (lyed, dyed, and laid to the side) hairdos. The time when Black life had value to Black folk, in spite of the confusion over the question of good hair (straight hair) versus bad hair (nigga hair, nappy hair). Drinking soda pop at a segregated lunch counter. He wonders why he didn't take his ass down the street to the black-owned diner on 30th St. The mean stares and dirty looks of the gray folk convinced him to never make such an undisciplined mistake again. He was not of the lot of knee-grows who felt it necessary to eat and shit where the gray folk did; he did not believe in the integration that would ultimately lead to the end of Black solidarity, struggle and love.

He thought of Marcus Garvey, and felt such shame at how the amerikkkan kneegrows were allowing their children's tomorrows to be sold—lock, stock, and barrel—by the backward, white want-to-be uppity kneegrows. With the streetcars moving slowly down Center St., he glanced into the store fronts of clothing and furniture stores that he could not go into. But he didn't wish to shop in such places—they didn't sell the sort of clothes that he or his homeboys would wear, not even in their caskets. He looked into the faces of the people that his people were being told were better than them, and he laughed. He could not help but laugh at the absurdity of it all. Feeling the uncaring eyes of those he laughed at bore into his back, he increased the volume of his soul-stirring laugh. They all continued on their way, thinking him a simpleminded and harmless teenage nigger.

He looked to the sky and noticed the oncoming rain-filled clouds, and picked up his pace as he walked along the railroad tracks—a short cut home. As he came to the closed-down steel mill—which went out of business last year—he thought he saw that which he hoped he didn't see. The mill, which was seven stories, sat on the edge of what was once a beautiful stream that he and his friends used to swim in when younger. There was a figure that moved on the rocky banks of the stream, a nude figure, a female figure. Had the figure been that of a black female, he wouldn't have been filled with the foreboding fear of doom, lynch mobs in white hoods, and hound dogs with foaming mouths. He tried to remove his eyes from the figure as he approached; he tried to curtail his movement towards the swimming figure, but his body would have none of it despite his fears and feelings of doom waiting and wanting it to happen.

He tried to return himself to the cage which he was dwelling at in the year 2000, but the 1959 mindslip would not cease. His eyes would not open. The gray girl began to move, sit up, and turn to look him directly in the eyes, with a smile of untold malevolence. As if her look had summoned him to come closer, his feet took him to her side. Standing over her, not speaking, just contemplating her pale frame, he grew erect, and she smiled. When he realized that she hadn't been gazing into his eyes, but at his groin, he began to groan in his mind—screaming a command of "run" to his legs and feet. There was no response.

Standing rooted where he stood, with erection straining to break free from the constraint of his wranglers, redhead lass he visited his dreams before, raised forth her hand to touch that which she gazed at with a look that could be called longing. As she did so, he found his right hand running through her wet hair. He thought himself insane! Still smiling, she caressed his erection with care, then with a roughness that caused him some discomfort. Yet, in spite of her roughness and his fear, with his free hand, he unbuttoned and zipped down his jeans. Coming to rest on his knees, at her side, they kissed a savage open-mouthed kiss. With her hands holding his erection, his hands still in her hair, their eyes burned into each other. It began to rain, and they made not love, but had mad intercourse.

Her eyes were green and gray, his brown. He remembered that she was the Irish lass, from the forest, through which the gods spoke to him. Still gazing into her eyes, both of them spent yet unsatisfied, he thought that in 1959 this wasn't going down, that this had to be another of Mary's tricks to pull him away from his mission, his search for the will to live. She still hadn't said as much as a word to him, and he still hadn't attempted to say a word to her. They just gazed into each other's eyes with longing and untold racial fantasy-induced malice, on the bank of a tream, in his dream, about both their worlds.

VI

daze-ee

I feel the undying need
to stretch forth
my hand
and touch your face,
as I sing the song
of love
and life to you.

I don't care if the
world cringes
in unholy disregard
for my song
that embodies
the tenets
of people's revolution
and
the ingredients
for the destruction
of capitalist man's
hold on the
hearts and minds
of those
who dare
move out
against him.

Yet,
these people,
who I sing for,
act as if

*they fear
the
internal struggle
required
of them
to raze
his humanity
crushing
world order,
that exist
within them.*

*I taste your fears,
as I lick away
your
salty tears of
sorrow and pain
of
having been
touched
by the
blighted minds
of the
dimwitted
fools
you
had given
yourself to.*

*Singing proud songs of
justice and equality,
mental struggle
and
spiritual healing,*

A DISJOINTED SEARCH FOR THE WILL TO LIVE

as I move
my body
and
my mind
to the beat of
your heart's song
of thanks
and praise
to the gods
for sending
me
your
way.

As
I pull
these words
from the very
depths of my
undying spirit
of rebellion,
I sense
your
unease with
my ease of grace
and care
at daring
to touch you
in a place
where the system's
educational frauds
had told you
didn't exist.

VII

Follow

It has been said by the romantics of old that one should follow one's heart; that one should dare to live and breathe the beautiful air of life. If you have the desire to love, to feel beyond the limiting boundaries of conservative society, then you must take heart and leap for the goal. Well, I am one who is from this age of profit over life, who has dared to attempt to be a man, in spite of being born into a world situation that was designed for the deprivation of such experiences. Though I have tasted fully the bitterness that such an inhuman world design compels one to digest, the world of the romantics has won out in this battle for my humanity over my inhumanity. My drive to be in love with life has given my being the basic outlet necessary to inform me of the fact that "that which has been imagined need not be forgotten" and that "if one struggles with daring, intestinal fortitude, and truth, those things which were but imaginations would become a reality outside of you." And for me this reality has not been forgotten, nor ignored. However, this is encumbered by the harshness of the world I was born into and had no part in creating. Such a world has placed many barriers before me and my kind of human being. Though any form of oppression and subjugation is deplorable, the fact that such a wicked and unjust system can exert the sort of oppressive control that not even the eternal life of love can escape. With the embellished hope of fabled but true heroes, I still launched forward to taste this succulent truth in spite of the abuse and misuse of having been born New Afrikan and true, in a land of united fools and extraordinary pretenders.

To mourn having been compelled to taste such bitterness is to be expected—it is O so very important that it is done for the sake of healing. Over the years I have cried much. I have cried big tears, small tears, and loud tears. But the majority of these tears were silent. The tears that are shed in the silence of one's heart and mind—the tears of the soul. I have witnessed the strongest of men break up, lose their nerve and ultimately their sanity, because they had failed to attempt to heal themselves via the shedding and sharing of tears with the world of their and other folks' souls. They didn't dare challenge the evil mannerisms of the venomous ones; they didn't believe in the mysterious and extraordinary tales of love told by the medieval romantic. I here speak of the romantics that gave birth to men such as Hannibal, the warrior-general who dared dream of victory against a foe militarily superior to his own—that is in terms of standing men, location, and entrenchment. But his love of his homeland, Carthage, was greater than his fear of defeat and death. And with such a deep devotion to his kind, his land, he set off to do battle with the strongest military force in the world. Yet for me, the resurgence of the romantic, the human consciousness of "that which has been imagined need not be forgotten," has brought victory to the defeat of those who went before me.

Through the creative genius of just being, these words of mine must be felt and thus expressed. The baseness from which love deferred springs cannot fully be verbalized with the limited image-shaping powers of the spoken or written word. This baseness can only be conveyed and understood through the powers of the human's capacity to think, reason, intuit via the instrument of being, of living. For me, as it was for the romantics, the power of intuition is at the forefront of the three human capacities. If the romantics of old were to witness such baseness, they may very well have changed their tune concerning following one's heart. For this age would surely erase from their pen hand the memory of their stories of love and sacrifice, honor and hope, innocence had in abundance and selfishness banished. They would probably die from massive heart cessation. I would perish with them, tumbling off to the world behind this one—the world told of by the dreamers and sages.

Concerned with this idea of "following one's heart," I have endeavored to bring this reality to bear in my interaction with the women in my life. I have loved greatly but have suffered the whip of disregard more times than I care to recall. Yet I have to remember each time. With unabashed precision I replay over and over, through my mind, which is shaped by the sensibilities of the warrior-priest, each lash of the whip that fell across my heart; each lash I endured without as much as a cry being uttered in rage or shame. With the purpose and intention of learning from each of these human interactions the lessons that will ensure the future protection of my warrior-priest heart and mind, I acknowledge the hurt and abuse that each and every woman in this country called amerikkka has suffered at the hands of each and every institution that makes up the system that runs the country. And secondly, I have to accept the fact that men and women both play a role in the continuation of social living. Not wanting to develop the insecure and enslaved disposition of my contemporaries, the modern day fool, I incessantly carry out my program of daring to question the assumed and propogated truths of this age concerning the relations of human being to fellow human being; woman to man and man to woman.

Taking heart, daring to be nonconformist; daring to ask the questions of he who fears not change, I travel the street of the warrior priest—spreading the message of open heart interaction with all those who have acknowledged, developed, and placed into practice their human capacities to reason, think, and intuit for the sake of healing themselves, and thus striving to assist the further advancement of humanity down the road of healing one another in their interaction with one another!

The romantic in this here sufferer just will not be shushed; I just will not be intimidated into capitulation to the sociopolitical, economic, or racial ways of the dominant cultural forces. I refuse to taste the sweet blight of the ways of the unjust order's manner of castigating the human earth that gave birth, life, and shape to his sorry ass. As man, as he without a name, I will pursue the promise of becoming the "new" man of the 21st century; the "new" man which is in reality the historical romantic man of old, Brave Heart and Tru! Dismissing the foul taste of the world order's stupidly proud man, I dare walk right up to the sun, hand in hand with my pride and love of the life of that other half of humanity that will continue to be the garden of all human life, the garden from which the beauty of all humanity will spring forth...Until I expire, I will continue to glide the interior of my essence, my inner sun, to taste and appreciate the fruit of her beauty, touch her heart, inform her mind, and enjoy her heaven; for I am the romantic man.

PART FIVE

I

*A caged cub turned
lion untamed, hating
each moment of his
separation from the
wild*

*Chewing and clawing
at that foe
which holds his body behind
concrete and steel*

*Concrete and steel
so high and so cold*

*Flashing his
asphalt and steel sharpened
teeth and claws
while choking on
his own spit and blood,*

*Raging on and warring on
growing impatient
for the embrace and kiss
of his beloved*

A DISJOINTED SEARCH FOR THE WILL TO LIVE

who awaits his return to
the wilds of the so-called
free world, to be
free at her side—
as he should be

Totally unsatisfied with
such an unjust waiting for
his chance to exhale
all the pain of living in exile,
in the belly of hell,
to inhale
the love and freedom that his
beloved one holds in abundance:

the ability
to
inhale Revolution!

Dear X,

I cannot tarry here very long...I just got what could be considered bad news—the Federal District Court just turned down/denied my petition for habeus corpus relief. Though I am not a bit surprised by the court's decision, I am however angered by the fact that I have to petition my adversaries' institutions of racist injustice for my stolen liberty—the very institutions that have taken it. This is the thing that bothers me most about this situation of repression, the fact that it holds me within its smothering grip of insanity, and dares call me criminal, biologically insane for my dark hue-man earth beauty. I grind my teeth as I write you this letter—listening to the Cure...trying not to be too mad (sometimes such music offers me a sort of escape from this draining experience). Though, I must admit that your letter has offered me a Tru reason to smile. I feel you totally...and before long you will be feeling me totally also.

I guess a part of me wishes to shed a tear. I mean I have to think of my Papa, who just passed away in one of these concentration camps, and all of my elders who informed me by their experience that I must ready myself to deal with the prospect of doing at least 8 more years in this hell...I am sorry! I do not wish for you to be touched by my sadness over having to swallow these sick people's self-serving bullshit. To them all of this is but a joke, but this is my life.

Here I would like to make a statement about the white/european male. I have come to the realization that the european male, and all who accept his world-view consciously or unconsciously, no matter his political, religious, or ideological position, will not change their dehumanizing white supremacist view of all life—that is all life except his own. I do not dare say that they do not have the capacity to do thus, but I will never refuse to look at the road he has taken us all down. I refuse not to look at his history of genocide and profit that has paved the way to the present destructive end that we and all of creation now witness via the reality of a many-layered experience of suffering...In short, they believe that their way is the only way, and if you dare question it then something must be wrong with you! Because, in his mind, he believes that he is the most rational and logical in all of creation. For many, this is a hard pill to digest. But history shows him to be the only creature capable of creating the world we now must struggle to dismantle within ourselves (our character-structures) and to the world around us (the empire). They each understand the role that this world order plays in making him the demigod to all of hue-manity. And very few are willing to denounce such privilege—history informs us of this fact also. None of this means that we are to not deal with white males, however, it is meant to inform us of the very crucial need for us to be able to realize and understand such mentalities and behaviors of those white males who we interact with, those we call friends, lovers, or comrades. This, Daisy, is a fact that very few of our kind are willing to acknowledge: he is unfit to be in any position of control. It will take many years for this mentality and behavior to be dealt with in any effective manner...And no I do not hate white males, I just have a very keen understanding of him and his insane design for all of hue-manity. The realities of this war, of what motivates this man, are very ugly and deadly. Before you can talk of fighting a war of liberation, you had better first have properly identified the enemy and his motives, strengths and weaknesses. This is the nature of the art of war!

It would be very nice of we could simply restrict the enemy to being just a faceless system, but this is not reality, this would not do anything but compel us to continue to play the same old song to a different tune. We have to take heart and dare to look the enemy in the eye! This doesn't in any way defer the love that we have for each other (this includes the white male), but it will defer the right of the few to rule our very hearts and minds; negate their power to twist and bend our powers to create our own reality; deny him control of our destiny.

Brave heart and true,
The man with no name.

II

So far removed from the ugliness of a world gone mad, only in his dreams was he able to dream of times past, live a life long dead to the senses of the folk who live in this time of the return of the she-devil. He thought often of Bill Gates and his billions in capital; he wondered why he cried so much, in sorrow and joy, over his own ability to touch the wind, smell the clouds, and love the life once begotten by the humanity now gone mad with the mindless fantasies created by Microsoft, Yahoo, and the Amazon absent the reality of life. He made love to himself often. He thought of Afrika always. He didn't hope the hope of the average person that dreamed and struggled to achieve the amerikkkan dream. He was a man who thought of freedom and bliss, love and life…but, yet and still none of this made sense in the age of isolation and anti-social internet use.

Still with the love of death hunting him, he ran through his own universe—a universe connected to the world of each and every living and past soul on this earth—he fell short, yet found his way. Calling out her name, "Brandy," he fell to the earth smelling of love and hope. Thinking of Bill Bradley and Al Gore, George Bush Jr. and the new 1000 year cycle of rage and pain. Struggling to be free of that thing that has left the world in a state of ugly-be-gone splendor. He stumbled and fell, but got back up. He loved Jane Fonda movies, but hated Jane Fonda's politics of leading niggas on a trail of everlasting tears of misguided hope and longing. He thought of Newton, Carter, Huggins, Clark, and Fred Hampton!

He loved the taste of Jack Daniels and Southern Comfort, but hated the ways of Jack and Jill, and the uncomfortable hospitality of the southland. Creeping in his sleep, drugged out over the lost times of Afrikan resistance and struggle to be free of that lie that now consumes our beautiful worlds, our only home in the universe of dead planets and black holes. Longing to taste the sweet and bitter of life in a society, a world, lost in the grip of technology, cyber space, and internet sex, he rolls off the end of his bed, drunk from the jailhouse wine made by his man Jay. Thinking that things had to turn around.

The Stock Exchange has no depressions or down-turns since the west's culture of death has achieved its aim of subverting the cultures of life the world over; no problems since 1992 and Saddam thought himself white enough to buck NATO and the UN. Growing tired of rolling on the floor of yesterday, he spits on the aim of the NAACP and its lost cause of turning black into white, and white into a love of the life that he can not have, a life free of truly working for a way that is free of the blood of the black, brown, red, and yellow that it needs to create its utopia absent the presence of people of color—people too dark to call white.

Feeling stuck, lost, and confused in a time of never can never look to the outer for the support necessary to go on trying to love and care about those other than himself, he spins off of the News Radio death of the really funny guy with the name of Heart, and the smile of a true comedian. Moving through the promise of a better world in 1996, then the loss of the beauty and strength of Tupac, the only and best of his generation. Tupac felt, he understood, the pain of those who were being denied and murdered by a society bent on living in a world full of lies and illusions of niggas being happy in spite of the pain and loss of identity and purpose.

He thought of Tupac and cried, not because anything was lost, but because everything was gained and affirmed in the murder of a child of Afrika who dared care and feel the loss, the insanity, and hope to be found in the past and the struggle to resist the illusion of inclusion in a society built on the blood of the children of Afrika, in New Afrika. He remembered, so he did not die too soon; he died in the time allotted to him by the Creator that breathed life into each and every soul on this plain of physical existence.

He remembered,
refused to forget,
Black Jesus!

TUPAC LIVES!

Thug life lives to
one day
transform
into
REVOLUTIONARY LIFE:

A LIFE DIRECTED
TOWARDS THE CREATION
OF A
LIFE DETERMINED TO
CREATE A SPACE
AND TIME
THAT AFFIRMS
AND EMBRACES
BLACK LIFE!

do or die;
ride or die,
the motto
and reality
for all
Black life
determined
to be free
to be
FREE!

III

Unless he say grace
he shall never be free again!

And
the disappointment
returned to him,
in his sleep,
in his dreams.

She,

Mary,
thought him weak,
but
knew him to be strong.

She
fed off of
the contradictions of life,
the contrarieties of existence
in a world
that could not
exist without
such a
dialectic.

IV

Man Identified Man

I am willing to be:
        Stronger than steel,
   yet soft as cotton.
        As brave as a lion,
   yet timid as a cat.
        Able to leap
   the moon in a single bound.
        Run through Klan
town in my dark skin,
with a heart full of moon
shine...Stop!

But what is all of the talk of undying courage, sweetness, and weakness? Is it not some sort of contradiction of mass proportion? Or is it just that this man writer is playing at being a man with woman tendencies? Is he some sort of confused homosexual, bent on being straight? Naw! Is there anything wrong with being gay? Naw!

Then what sort of man is this, for whom does he claim such capabilities? Is it for woman, that cursed lot of male stupidity, that he dares make such stupendous claims, such suave declarations? Well of course, and on and on, I dare claim demo, in earnest, my stunning abilities of practicing that which flies in the face of the absurd practice of the 21st century male!

"Who am I?"—you may be asking
yourself...wondering how I can
dare claim to be thus...
Well I am unabashed man,
of course! Unabashed by the
evils of paternalism, capitalist
man's justification of the enslavement of the world.

I am man identified man.
Man who openly defines his self
as he who dares not chain
another to himself for the sake
of ego, profit, or false advertisement:
Delusions of grandeur.

Naw, none of that. I be just a
New Afrikan man of maternalistic
ancestry, almost destroyed by caveman's world view, in a guise of holy,
Christ-like, god sent, matrimony
of manifest destiny.

A DISJOINTED SEARCH FOR THE WILL TO LIVE

I be resurrected man in his
natural state. Free from the
fetters of imperialistic cultural
trappings of boorish amerikkkan
masculinity, and his New World
order schemes in the mask of
world peace.

Still not clear as to who
I be? Let us try this
again...

Just as a man trapped, chained,
to the hate of Skeleton Bay,
Alcatraz, Marion design of
"SS," Gestapo, Willie Lynch's
genocidal mind, with profit
as the grand prize.

A New Afrikan man, raped
at the age of six, branded
retarded at the age of nine,
called useless at the age of 12,
banned from all schools at 14,
charged as a rapist at 16,
and shoved into prison, raped
yet again at 17 and 18,
dying to be free of all pain
at 19, reclaim life at 20.
Seeking justice at 21,
from racist charges and
a cold hearted
push into a guilty plea by a
system bent on killing

me. At 27, still charged
as a rapist, but there will
be no more rape of me:
He who dares to be
Superman for my woman,
Mother Earth, and all of humanity.

Feel me? Yes indeed, I am a romantic with the nerve to create a reality beyond that which presently maked waste of the red tailed hawk, open meadows, tree covered hillsides, and rain forests teeming with life yet to be seen.

I be man identified man.

V

Split

There is a tear
in the fabric
of humanity's
soul
a hole in the denims
of the earth's ozone
blue layer.

Coming apart at
its seams,
we find the world
being ripped asunder
by big ugly machines,
eroded by
unnatural waste,

A DISJOINTED SEARCH FOR THE WILL TO LIVE

and negated
human invalidation.

Such a tear cannot
go unmended

Wearing its rugged
and trial worn
blue jeans,
we witness the
simultaneous razing of
the universe's finest
creations: the earth
and its inhabitants.

There's a split
in the sky, a
hole in man's heart,
and no damn sense in
his caveman head;
a head empty
of the sense
he was
endowed with.

Man moves
to erase himself
from the memory of
that force which said "Be"
and we all were
and looked to the sky
counting stars and
constellations,
until we lost the whole

and split into
the fools and simpletons
that rule and obey...

And all seem
to refuse
to say,
"this split shit needs to
be mended!"
with each of us daring to
sport the blue jeans of
humanity
embellished with the breast
plate of brave heart and tru
concern of the muthafuckin
next persons right to
breathe, to sing, to be as
their own humanity would
have them be: protectors and
maintainers of the blue jean
wearing atmosphere that surrounds
our world.

VI

Singing and dancing in the streets with Mick and David, making a farce of revolutions, riots, and rebellions, against oppressions and exploitation of the worst kind, he thinks of having sex with a Grace Jones look-alike; while eating grapes off the back of a saint bernard in Paris. Promising himself to remember always the promise he made to jewel to keep the faith in his own ability to make change for a twenty, though he knows not how to count past 1999. Y2K bugs promised to touch off the second coming of she who loves horseradish and cornflakes afer sex; it didn't come, but made all the store merchants richer, the poor blind, and the crimes of the stock exchange rage on in Times Square, with the falling of the ball, which brought in the new century with more white lies of capitalism's grand victory over the uncertainty of the primitive.

It's a sin, it's a crying shame to think that he thought himself redeemed because he could talk with himself, and be held responsible for failing to call attention to the atrocities of the past, of today and the days to come. In Afrika, his homeland, he watched as his kind lived without water and a place to lay their heads, while the invaders of various shades of gray installed the kneegrows they wanted in charge of the affairs of the state, as they stole and robbed the backward jungle bunnies of their minds, their children, their future. In amerikkka, he still felt himself free. The stupid nigga still thought himself Afro-American! He is so depressed, so sad! He *did* try! He still thought himself somehow capable of shaking the white man within him. He had to accept certain realities about his socialization, certain realities that could not be denied. He had to live with the ugliness of the ways of the truly primitive; he had to acknowledge that the blues that he had lived and suffered were brought to him, that his pain was the creation of this cultural love affair that existed between Mary and himself. That idea created by Babylon, the she-devil as Mary, is the reality of amerikkka, of technology, of progress, of a pale utopia via prosperity brought on by dead niggas, spics, chicks, and other darkies the world over. The murder of pale folks' souls accounts for the greatest success of Babylon "the great."

He wished he knew what he was looking for—was it something shimmering and white? Was he looking for that which was black and proud? Or was his soul doomed to explore the land of never can never be free to taste that which is not shimmering and white? Under the milky way, this night, he gazed off into the direction where man first saw the gods approach the earth's blue glow of water. He was determined to go dance with the wolves and buffaloes long dead since the lost souls of the senseless pale invaders debased that which they called primitive. Cheikh Anta Diop told him to keep moving towards the love of freedom and struggle, that had gotten him this far in spite of the invader's drive to smoke his ashes at a dinner party in the Abe Lincoln room of the white house. He thought Diop insane, for he wanted to fight, but didn't know how. His looking and searching continued beyond the light of the rising sun.

PART SIX

I

...education: a mutual process, world mediated; man as an uncompleted being, conscious of his incompletion, and his attempt to become more fully human.
—Paulo Freire

Dear X,
I have a few important thoughts that I would like to share with you. Love and revolution go together like peanut butter and jelly, like playgrounds and cartwheel tires. You cannot have one without the other. Now when it comes time to define these two concepts the problems begin. Love means certain things to certain people, as does revolution. How we define and live love and revolution will determine the face of the sort of struggle that we wage. What are we struggling for—what sort of community, society, world? I do not believe that it is enough to simply say that I love humanity and that I am fighting for the revolution. These concepts have to be defined, stated, and pursued once a definitive consensus has been reached by all those involved. I mean if we are to be taken seriously, we must first start taking ourselves seriously. What is it exactly that we are supposed to be fighting against? Is this enemy real or imagined, weak or strong? What role does love play in our individual and collective lives?

Now, for me love and revolution are not relative terms. These are two absolute truths in the reality of human existence. However, these two, one which completes the other, become relative when we begin to deal with the step by step, context to context, environmental, cultural, sociopolitical, and economic differences of those who may dare speak and carry out such profound ideas in the service of humanity, in the name of unselfish devotion and authentic respect. In your last letter you stated that "we seem to be on the same boat in our world-view and our analysis of it, although we both have had different experiences." Now, based on what I have stated above about love and revolution, do you believe still that it is possible for you and I to share the same world-view? Is it possible for you and I to propose the same approach to engaging capitalist man based on the same analysis, given the fact that we have had different experiences? I ask you these questions because I desire only for you and I to arrive at a basic understanding of what it is that we are dealing with in each other. When we do get to the heart and soul of the problems that have been imposed on us and our world, what I see, the thing that I understand above all else, is that our experiences are very important to us coming to an understanding of each other. When we strip away the class, socioeconomic, differences, we will find the ugly face of our shared enemies. However, we first have to acknowledge the fact that his way of life is our enemy. The way he educates, perceives life, talks, walks, and thinks presupposes his right to subjugate the world to his twisted little boy's view of how we are all supposed to live.

If you were to read Kant, Hume, Locke, Plato, Hegel, and any other of the so-called great thinkers of europe, what you will find, if you know what you are reading, is the battle between these men of how they were going to succeed in despiritualizing and dehumanizing humanity. They always spoke of absolute and relative truths. They theorized on the universality of the truth, knowledge, and any other human difference that needed to be negated as invalid because it wasn't european. From Hegel to Lenin the dialectics, the revolutions, the international communist this and that was in reality the same thing Locke and all the other capitalist parasitic thinkers were proposing: the domination of european culture, thought, and practice; white supremacy and nationalism. The Russians did to the Indigenous Asian tribes/Nations of the largest part of its land base, which is in Asia, the same thing that their brothers did to the indigenous people here in the amerikkkas, south afrika, israel, new zealand, australia, and any other part of our planet where you might find him outside of europe—he placed them in chains first, colonized them and purged them, then colonized the minds of those who would not die. This is the main reason for Lenin speaking of the "oppressed nations' right to self-determination." In truth he and his party feared a full rebellion, a revolution, by the internal colonies of imperial father russia.

I have said all that to make the point that it isn't our differences in experiences that should hinder us from realizing our need to rally together. Though each situation that we will confront will differ in the manner in which we will need to approach it, it is more important for us to come to the basic understanding that if we are fighting for the right of all life to live and breathe without fear of being slain, placed in a concentration camp for profit, or catching cancer, we will have to see that that which threatens these lives threatens all of our lives in the final analysis. It is not our differences in appearances or gender that should present themselves as a barrier to our being able to love, grow and develop as family, friends, comrades, or lovers; it is the ideas, the world-views, the ideological dispositions that should be the determining factor in our interactions, and should remain thus. For if I am fighting for justice and you are fighting for the system's right to be unjust, then we are mortal enemies for life, forever, for eternity.

Now, you need to understand that I am one New Afrikan who knows that I am the reject of the rejected; that my life means absolutely nothing in the eyes of the system of those who are my so-called people. I have tasted the lash a million times on every level of this existence and in every sense that is real. Yet, I do not cringe at my duty to rise above all of these forces that seek to push me out of this existence. No, never that! This is why I have developed the patience of the lone wolf: I lay back, awaiting the chance to strike my foe down; my foe who feels himself to be the hunter, but knows not that in fact he is the prey...and, still I rise!

None of what I have said above is meant to negate the fact that we all do have a great work to carry out within our individual selves, but our struggle to relieve ourselves of the cultural, psychological, emotional, intellectual, vocational, and spiritual fetters of capitalist man cannot, no never, be done alone. Here's where the differences in experience present the greatest barrier to our kind's unity. Here's where the degree of suffering and ease comes in as a veil of illusions designed to have each of us hate on each other. You get the actual promise of a good job, home, car, and social status, whereas I get nothing but empty and unfulfilled promises...you get college, I get the cage. But the blight that besets your existence is so insidious and deadly that its existence is often missed by those of your experiences. I cannot help but miss them, I am of the caste of untouchables. Before I was born, before I was even conceived, my future was being mapped out by those in high places. I was marked for a living death long before I could even take two steps. The environment in which I developed my outlook on this life was designed to give life to an inferior take on myself and the larger world, in my mind and heart. But I revolted, I dared feel, I dared call myself a man, a human being...and this is where you are at: in full revolt!

I am not supposed to be the man that I am today! This system murders those of my kind, outright, on every level of this existence, of this life. Simply because they understand that the illusions, the lies, the bribes and fears have no sway over my will, my determination, to be free. Once I came to life spiritually, intellectually, and emotionally, he knows that Sun Yzu, Shaka Zulu, Queen N'Zinga, Nat Turner, and John Brown come to life within me; he knows that I will remember the Middle Passage, the Boxer Rebellion, the Trail of Tears, the Dawn of Time, but more importantly, the Beauty and Right to life of all Life! I am the foe that he dreads the most. Yet, it is so important for me to remember that I must never allow him to know my intentions, my abilities, or my strength...I must remain simply a broke nigga in his mind. When I say him, I am speaking of anything or anyone who believes in the system and is willing to fight and die for the system of white male domination...I will have to explain that more in some future communication—preferably face to face.

Having come to terms with my incompleteness, my weaknesses and infirmities has driven me more towards developing myself as a man. Each day that I spend in this inhuman condition compels me to witness the absurdity of this existence. I am not just talking about the obvious absurdity of existence in these sort of places—I see the total picture—I am talking about all of what we call society, the absurdity of society. We can talk of politics, cultural matrixes, or social voids, but none of this sort of intellectual jargon could even scratch the surface of the absurdity which besets all our lives.

All dialogue on the matter, the problems, is necessary. However, we must always begin at the point, the starting gate, of the human face of the problems. We must never attempt to remove human suffering from the equation of any sort of revolutionary analysis of the cause of human suffering, the antithesis of human well-being and continuation. Marx, Lenin, and all of the so-called people's thinkers have given the world a legacy of stupidity, a legacy of european thought that negates reality. What is required today is a new way of thinking, seeing, and acting upon the world, in unison with the world as it acts upon us in return. The dialectical materialism of Marx, the leftist, the anarchist, and the other so-called deep thinkers that deal with "thesis, antithesis, and synthesis," negate much of the reality, and all of the spirit of humanity—they have no idea of the human face of the thesis, the base nature of the antithesis, thus their synthesis always falls short of creating that which is supposed to negate the ugly reality of capitalist man's insane world order. Progress and order, technology and commerce, trade and tariff, and middle class values and ambitions drive the slaves on every class and caste level in this society, this absurd arrangement, yet knowing this, they still produce bullshit, settler/colonial centered theories and plans of action...The point being that I am driven by this need to never deny the ugly reality of this unjust order, but at the same time I know that the manner in which I attack it will be limited just by virtue of my lowly status in this class/race based society. As strong as I am, I have to acknowledge this weakness, my weakness, created by our enemy. We need to be protecting and valuing each other's lives...My kind and I cannot do this alone. But no one seems to understand this, in spite of what our history has shown us. But so-called "conscious revolutionaries" fear the momentous duty that our history has placed on our shoulders...yet we must move on regardless of their faint-hearted inaction, which is masked as being "rational and patient maneuvering." Fuck 'em! Yet, I know that we will have to work with them and trust them as far as we can see them.

I will here break from my above ranting and raving, smile! I mean, let us both smile and be real. It is nice or safe to be serious all of the time. I make attempts to find ways to relieve my mind of the stress and strain that comes along with consciousness, love, and vision, while being held captive in an inhuman environment of profit and genocide. It is far from being an easy task. I do wish to share with you that part of me that I am restricted from exposing and expressing for the sake of survival. The average person in my life has not a clue as to the level and depth of my love, humanity, and spirit of resistance. The fact is that they couldn't give a flying fuck as to my sense of deep love of life and people. They have been scarred so deeply themselves, they have been taught how not to think and feel, their human eyes have been closed to even their own suffering. I dare not attempt to pull back the veil of illusion that covers their mind's eye. Here I am talking about the folk who are in the so-called free world. I cannot even point out the beauty of breathing to them—they would think me mad if I dared do such. I at times find myself wanting to grow cold, to not feel, because of the sadness that often besets my heart and mind. I cringe at these thoughts and feelings, yet I understand them to be the product of 27 years of nonstop racist injustice and economic depression. I run through the corn fields of my mind, trying to steady myself, trying to center my confusion and pain over having to yet spend another day in this hell.

I have said too much, and must move on to answer these other letters. Take care.

Relentlessly,

The Sun King.

II

Dear Comrade,

I hope that this letter finds you well. I be still here, in chains, trying acutely to remain sane. The vile psychological and emotional effects I must endure, caused by this prison/neoslavery existence, is one of the most feared weapons in our enemy's arsenal of pestilence and genocide. These years and days spent in isolation and exile, separated from family, from friends, from freedom; forced to miss the struggle of my family in that same society that separated us; the dehumanizing scars inflicted on the minds of those of us who are reduced, negated, and equated to the subhuman status of our forebears who were made the victims of european economics (capitalism); made to submit to a repressive situation supposedly designed to correct so-called criminal behavior, while in fact what is occurring is the further erosion and deforming of the naturally ordered social inclinations endowed in the marrow of all human beings. The question of my humanity, my right to life, liberty, and the quest for human purpose, has been answered by the call of monopoly capital to destroy such human rights for their bestial lust to accumulate super profits via the criminalization of my kind of human being.

Such blatant and insidious disregard and discard are the incessant realities that I must daily confront, combat, and conquer; such insanity chips away at the resolve of the strongest of my kind…Simply put…I am doing okay simply because I am alive, still struggling to become more fully human, in spite of the situation.

As to your proposal to reactivate the Prisoner Solidarity Committee (PSC) formation within the Anarchist Black Cross Federation, I think that you should continue to push it, however, I do not wish to become involved in it. My reason for not wanting to be involved is because I do not agree with the idea of any New Afrikan being a social prisoner. I have (as have many other revolutionary New Afrikans as well) long ago come to recognize the political reality that each and every New Afrikan in this settleristic-imperialist nation is in fact a prisoner of war, and once we are shoved in this situation of acute repression we become political prisoners of war. Historically speaking, the war that I am indirectly making reference to began when european capital launched its first slave ships and began its free market system with the trade of my Afrikan forebears. At the conclusion of the amerikkkan war for independence, the present capitalistic nation-state called the USA was founded for euroamerikkkans, but my kind remained in chains.

The constitution was written by and for the euroamerikkkan's right to determine and govern themselves as human beings. But my kind, my forebears, remained the chattel of settleristic amerikkka. In this constitution our subhuman status was affirmed and reaffirmed by those who wrote it. They defined them as being three-fifths of a person in this very constitution that is hailed as being the greatest ever written. In 1857, the highest court of law in the USA (the supreme court) again affirmed the status of "subhuman slaves" of my kind, in the court's

Dred Scott decision. US Chief Justice Roger Brooks Taney said, "a Negro has no rights that a white man is bound to respect." To show their correctness and legal grounds for denying the slave Dred Scott's petition for freedom, the United States Supreme Court turned to the Constitution written by their fathers for their freedom to oppress and profit from the genocide and enslavement of the Native and Afrikan slave, and said:

> When the Constitution and the Declaration of Independence were written, Africans were perceived as three-fifths of a person. When one speaks of "we the people," we were not speaking of you. And therefore we cannot now give you the rights and appurtenances that apply to "we the people." The Constitution has no relevance to you and your kind, or to your descendants should they ever become free.

The whole system/institution of slavery was an act of war that was committed against the nations within Afrika which the european slavers (from europe and the amerikkkas) captured, bought, and sold their victims. The nations of europe waged this war in the name of capitalism, civilization, and christianity. These Afrikan human beings had never before encountered such a foe that came in the disguise of a friend and trader of pretty and shiny products, thus they were not prepared for the deceit, betrayal, racism, greed, and hate that motivated these pale men.

New Afrikans were supposedly freed on December 6, 1865 by the 13th amendment to the US Constitution, which reads: "Neither slavery nor involuntary servitude, except as a punishment for crime whereof the party shall have been duly convicted, shall exist within the United States, or any place subject to their jurisdiction." And almost three years later on July 9, 1868, we were compelled to accept the paper citizenship ratified by congress in the 14th amendment of the constitution, which reads "All persons born or naturalized in the United States and subject to the jurisdiction thereof, are citizens of the United States and of the State wherein they reside. No State shall make or enforce any law which shall abridge the privileges or immunities of citizens of the United States; nor shall any State deprive any person of life, liberty, or property, without due process of law; nor deny to any person within its jurisdiction the equal protection of the laws."

With the ratification of these amendments came much fanfare and praise by those Kneegrows who claimed to have been the representatives of the New Afrikan masses whose true desire was to be liberated from the nation-state that held the captives as slaves, a country that had robbed them of their human right to self-determination and independence as a Nation. The student of history will surely see that all these laws that have been enacted and ratified by the capitalist and white supremacist judicial and legislative body of the US government, for the sham freedom granted to New Afrikans, was in reality no more than a political ploy used to further the interest of capital and white supremacy (which was and is simply to control and profit). Thus through the 13th and 14th amendments we recognize the fact that over 130 years ago the grounds for the prison industrial complex were laid. In both amendments the person could not be made a slave and deprived of life and liberty unless they had been duly convicted of a crime. As the children of the only people who were brought to this settleristic-imperialist nation in chains, we (I) realize that we are the victims of this undeclared war, and that history is not a dead thing, for all that is today is but a continuation of what has occurred those 130 years ago, that we are a colonized people. We have been bounded to this decadent nation through the laws, miseducation, and acute genocidal repression that has been waged against our nation.

I am simply trying to give you an idea of why I refuse to ever be a part of anything done by ABCF. As a New Afrikan, I do not accept or respect or recognize the legitimacy of the US government, nor the definition of the United Nations of what or who is to be defined as a Political Prisoner/Prisoner of War. My people, no matter how much they have been brainwashed, are all PP/POWs, simply because their continued exploitation and oppression are perpetuated by and through the political system of this capitalist nation. The conditions that give life to the so-called social crimes are created by this government. The Iran/Contra drug smuggling and the CIA crack cocaine pipeline into south central LA are but two very minute examples of how these situations are created by the government for economic forces/capital. I will not be confined to the definitions handed down by my oppressors, the very european nations that have created the blighted conditions that are killing millions of the world's people daily.

The definitions that ABCF are using do not take into account the present anti-colonial/revolutionary struggles that are being waged throughout this settleristic/imperialist nation. The new form and shape of our struggle is not even taken into consideration by this ABCF. They look to the comrades who have been locked down for over 20 years, who were engaged in the movement 20-30 years ago for insight into that which they could not possibly understand. The conditions that gave rise to the New Afrikan revolutionaries of my generation are conditions that are quite different from those that gave life to the brothers and sisters from our revolutionary struggles of the 60s and 70s. The government had effectively razed the revolutionary movement of that period in time. My generation was raised without the knowledge of that phase in our struggle for a full and complete freedom: self-determination and independence from this decadent capitalist nation-state.

My friend, the fact that ABCF is made up of middle class white folk is another reason for me and the Spirit Collective not wishing to be involved in such a federation. For to allow such a federation to set the terms of how we are to view who is considered PP/POWs is to section false internationalism. And we will not be part of this sort of endeavor.

Though we agree that the support of those brothers and sisters who have been targetted and framed by the government for the active roles they played in attempting to make revolution should receive the full support of the movement; we, however, simply do not see them as the only political prisoners and prisoners of war, solely because they made a conscious effort to engage this system of white supremacy and monopoly capital that oppresses and exploits and murders its internal and external neocolonies.

I hope that you will keep on struggling in the name of humanity and revolution. Though I do believe that we should create a united front for the making of the revolution for a better tomorrow, however, again, I will not be a part of any front that does not address the reality of white supremacy, the blight of all humanity.

Take care. Dare to struggle to dare to win!

Relentlessly,

Shaka N'Zinga.

III

Genocide is Okay

Opinion #1

Nigga,
ain't nobody trying
to hear that shit!
Fuck Mumia!
That nigga need to die!
Shit,
afterall,
he did kill a police officer?

Opinion #2

If Mumia need to die,
so do the rest of us.

Opinion #3

Well,
shit,
the rest of us
is dying already.
So fuck it!

Opinion #4

Yeah,
fuck it!
Why give a fuck?

Opinion #5

I can't think
of no reason
for concern.

Opinion #6

Pass me
that
joint,
fool!

PART SEVEN

I

Smiling faces in dangerous places;
Places plagued by grimy hands,
dirty pastors, and spaded nuns.

Trembling hands in the empty pockets
of soiled pants, skirts, and underwear.

Missing the end of a birth, grabbing
a hold of the cord of life, ending the
movement of hatred of self and kind.

Doing time in a concrete and steel box,
smelling of unwashed body parts, thinking
the end is near.

Not daring to miss the place in time where
the love of life was never lost; that place
being the place of the soul, the mind's eye,
where the truth of justice and liberty
forever resides.

When standing on a corner, one chilly spring evening, I saw up in the star-clustered sky an image of a woman's sex. With her clitoris standing erect as a man's confused manhood, this image of female heaven spoke to me, beseeching me to honor and respect her, to bow to her, to love all of her.

I could not help but laugh to myself, thinking: "That weed smoke sure was good. I gotta get more of that shit from Big Slim—the whiteboy from Rose Street." The female phenomenon winked at me, in such an erotic and provocative manner, causing me to grow as hard as a week-old bowl of welfare cheese, left behind the stove in a homemade rat trap.

Doing the business of providing a service to the needy dark masses of ghetto youth, old folk, and hard heads, I continued to serve my euphoric toxins in spite of the optical delusion that held my essence in a trance. I could smell the captivating scent of this female wonder up in the heavens. From that corner, surrounded by a hell not of my father's creation, I could taste her sweetness a billion miles from her station far beyond the disfigured reality that consumed all that was the nature and beauty of life. She called for me, inviting me to make love to her with my true manhood—the essence of me, the spirit-man.

But I misunderstood the depth of her request—I mistook her invitation for a physical act called "fucking." I missed the mark. She laughed in my face, at my male thing, after I had exposed it for all the world to see. She called it worthless but for the purpose of injecting the needed seed of life. I was confused. Quickly stuffing my wounded pride back into my pants, I questioned her rejection of me—she just stared at me.

With unmarked pig cars passing by, the junkies trying to cop from me though they were short a dollar or two, and my homies not paying me no mind, I stood on that corner, under a streetlight that didn't provide light, in front of a mailbox that the mailman never dared check, thinking to myself that this wasteland had become the mating ground of the universe. I stared heaven-bound, dumbfounded by the splendor of the woman who lived among the stars. I felt shame for calling my woman, my Boo, a bitch; for turning naïve college girls out on this shit called coke, for daring to curse my mother for not having a lot. I cringed in fear at the possibility of never having a chance to show my Boo my true manhood.

The shame of years of being a monster to the women of earth drove me back to the present, pulling me away from my true nature, my true self that had been abused by an order that profited from the debasement of true manhood/womanhood relationship. I shook and questioned the reality of what just occurred to me. I left the corner running, leaving behind me a mass of dark faces mad from the hunger for death as a means to escape from the starvation of life. I ran to my Boo's house, out of breath, I entered her front door, up the stairs that led to her room, pushing through the door, and stopping only to stare upon her naked sleeping form. Moving to the foot of her bed, in a room with walls covered with photos of her and me smiling and dancing, bonding and laughing, I looked upon her, and the thoughts of past wrongs, disrespect, and abuse filled my spinning and befogged consciousness. I dropped to my knees filled with the grief of having committed an unforgivable wrong.

I remembered the night in the park—a moonless, very cool summer night—when over a fence we climbed, into a forbidden place, to have our fill of each other. But she wouldn't let me do as I would with her— no brown eye this night; for there was not time for her to clean herself up properly. But I became enraged, with no understanding, just full of lust and selfishness—I left her there alone. Knowing full well that she would be unable to climb the fence by herself. She was arrested for trespassing; but in spite of this cowardly offence, she forgave me, and still I continued my selfish and stupid behavior.

Not having the courage nor the strength to speak, I closed my tear-filled eyes to take a look within, for the woman wonder in the sky, in the universe of my soul. Finding her, I asked her to forgive me and to be assured that I now overstand her meaning, her essence. Never again

A DISJOINTED SEARCH FOR THE WILL TO LIVE

would I be as I was towards women. For *the negation of woman is a negation of myself, of man, trembling.*

She touched my heart,
unless I say grace,
I shall never be free again.

He is Mr. Pitiful, like Otis Redding sang about, like the millions of his kind lived before him, like those of his generation, the children of a time wherein he sees the blood spilt, the lives wasted and stolen, he cries too much. He has no idea about being Mr. Happiness, like Bill Cosby plays at being, though he knows his life means shit in spite of his millions. He still talks to himself, chasing rainbows, refusing to live the acceptance of the lies told by those pale folk in control. Taking antidepressants to try to hold on to some form of reality. Nightmares in the daytime, daydreams in the nighttime, congested smoke-filled lungs, and he still thinks "Black Power" to be just around the corner.

Holding on to nothing but hope, Mr. Pitiful gets drugged about the times when he played the alto sax and handed out panther party flyers for self-defense on the street corners of Baltimore, back when black folk still loved that which was black; the times when the Blackman had the respect and love of his woman and children, because they understood that he was trying to win back the freedom denied them all. Mistakes were made, he understands this, but to continue to play at being like him, to try and outdo him in a system designed by him for him and his own, is absurd and self-defeating.

Back and forth, winning then losing, fighting some things and not trying to fight other things at other times, he finds himself sitting in the corner of his cage talking to himself about the insanity of even attempting to love a people that don't give a flying fuck about the memory of their ancestors, their children, or their own sorry-ass selves...but maybe there was hope to be found in himself, hope beyond the empire of global capitalism. Maybe from out of his bipolar state of concentration camp suffering he could bring to an end the journey that has taken him full circle back into the arms of Mary.

He smoked a joint, popped a fistfull of assorted blue and red pills, rested his head on the porcelain shit eater, and went off to REM slumber. Driven, driven, hounded and vilified by a state of affairs comfortable with the murder of the world for sake of its cowardly play at progress and harmony. He grabbed the ruins of his past lives, remolded the truth out of the lies told of his history, his past, and gave it the life and truth of the present need to validate that which has been denied. Jurisprudence in amerikkka is questioned only when the pale benefactors of genocide are affected harmfully by it, yet the destruction of the Afrikan child in himself never is to expect such a just consideration.

He is driven to depths, within himself, beyond the illusions of inclusion and racial progress, to a place that dares question and answer the truths of his own ability to rise above the farce of amerikkkan jurisprudence. He just had to sail the seas of that which she cannot take from him, his genetic memory of past reality experienced, never to be forgotten. Back and forth, driven from the past to the present through to the future, he's driven to dream.

II

In the state of self-pity, dreams, he is driven to the chained body of a man (who had hours before just been with his wife and children; whose odor was still fresh in his mind) being herded aboard the slave ship Jesus with many others who had the look of so much pain upon their beautiful faces; faces so full of humanity in grief, in sorrow of the savage bondage they found themselves being driven into. No one spoke or screamed, but in their hearts burned an eternal flame of resistance that was going to occur within them all, until the last of

A DISJOINTED SEARCH FOR THE WILL TO LIVE | 126

them all last stood.

Driven to witness death dressed in pale skin, with his Bible/Quran in hand, tricking Afrikans out of their right to life, liberty, and the pursuit of happiness, stood on the banks of the amerikkkas waiting to work his white magic on the minds of the new arriving free men, women, and children in chains. His plans were to erase, from the children of paradise, the memory of themselves as free and self-determining people, to make themselves, and to have their children's, children's, children's, weep and moan, to the children of the destroyer of their sanity, for their freedom.

Driven to see the results of these human beings' resistance to this paleman's savage criminal assault against their humanity, on the floor of the Atlantic ocean, in the bellies of sharks, crabs, and other grilled animals, he counted the remains of about 100,000,000 murdered—the remains of the warrior woman who refused to be raped, the warrior men who refused to stand by and watch, and the innocent future arriors, the children, who succumb to sickness and negation.

Driven to see Afrikans being chased through woods, rivers, and meadows by man-hunting dogs—for reaching for their freedom; for resisting slavery.

Driven to see Afrikan men hanging by their necks from trees, castrated, burning alive, with a pack of savage palemen, women, and children looking on, with much hatred in their eyes, as they smiled, laughed, and picnicked with the unmistakable scent of burning human flesh in the air. Not far away from this scene of eauroamerikkkan festivity, hung an Afrikan woman, raped and mutilated (the wife of the castrated burning man), with her stillborn child lying at her feet; with the look of dignity and disgust still radiating from her open eyes—murdered for reaching for their freedom; for resisting pale insanity.

Driven to see Afrikan children, women, and men lying dead in the streets, abandoned houses, and alleys with needles sticking out from their arms, crack pipes in their hands, and suicides on the bedroom night stands, gunshot wounds to the head with smoking gun being held in the hand of one who is an Afrikan "himself," with self-hate and confusion in his eyes—all the victims of the US so-called war on drugs, but it's genocide that it all spells in the end for these Afrikans in his driven dream!

In small rooms, in cages, he was driven to see confined Afrikans, believing themselves free, with TVs, radios, fans, word processors, three meals, and all that has given them a sense of ease which will in the end spell the complete acceptance of their kind's status as amerikkkan neoslaves—the result of a complete disregard and/or ignorance of their forebears' resistance, struggle, sacrifice, and death so that they may one day be free of all that they now seem to view as being a natural state for their kind of human being.

And they were all Black like me.

He's black like me, with Kiss and Ozzy tattooed on his fingers. He bobs his head to the tunes of Bob Dylan his favorite song is "Hurricane"—and he is Black like me. You know that cat is really into the melancholy songs of the Cure and the Smashing Pumpkins—he would marry Robert Smith if he was a woman—and he's black like me. He dances to the Bee Gees and cries to Karen Carpenter's "Rainy Day Mondays"—and he's Black like me. He's Black like me; a child of the ghetto ways. A child of Afrikan descent, born in amerikkka, lost in the process of socialization into hatred of self.

He's Black like me, he sings Curtis Mayfield songs as he struggles to grapple with the ugly facts of life in the colonial streets of Baltimore. No food, before Tupac, shooting dice, settling for the shrimp fried rice from the Chinese sub shop. Black like me, he finds his way out of the

Black slums, into the white slums, wandering about, making fake friends, aware of the evil socialization that they had been subjected to; a socialization that has left them insensitive to his humanity; that has them view him as if he was some sort of Paris World Fair novelty.

He learned to trust them as far as he could see them, though he saw the beauty in them, their ignorance of his humanity made him remain aware of their great potential to bring pain to his sanity. He learned the hard way, almost costing him his life, not to trust those who did not respect his existence as a human being, as an Afrikan. They got him drunk one night, they murdered and raped someone, but when the police got involved, he who is Black like me found himself in the hell designed to twist and bend his young 16 year old, arrested development mind and body—fast the tune of "the nigger did it" was being played in the minds and hearts, the media and the streets, when he found himself shoved in jail.

In hell he learned of the mistakes of the Moors in Spain, their trust in the equality afforded all who resided there, ultimately led to the undoing of their 800 year democratic rule, and they were Black like me. They did not understand the drive of that male of europe, the drive to have the black-a-moor bent and broken at his pale feet. The Moors failed to understand that justice and equality meant nothing to a group of people who craved to dominate and control the world peopled by folk Black like me.

That a world-view that would allow for the fair and just respect and chance at life for all, regardless of race, creed, or religion, meant nothing to those folk whose world-view okays lying, cheating, rape, murder, and genocide for the sake of controlling and enslaving those who attempted to create a world that expressed the reality of humanity's natural inclination towards the creation of a civilization, a world-order, free of hunger and poverty, oppression and exploitation, war and genocide, white supremacy and capitalism.

Black like me, he enjoyed the music of the world, the sound that brought life and sight to the indignities of being born Black like me in a world designed for folk white like you.

III

He thought
of Oprah
as
April Summertime,

and

April Summertime,
was a lady caught up
in driving miss daisy,
without a moral code,
to a Party of Five,
in the fable town
of Mayberry.

Tasting
the quickening
of life
after death,
shouting slogans
that showed
her own backwards,
Full House
thinking.

She,
a wanna-be ofay.

A DISJOINTED SEARCH FOR THE WILL TO LIVE

standing to sail
off to
better days
minus the
Black man—
hoping he pass away
by twelve midnight,
taking nothing
with him;
no pride,
style,
or whole,
unbroken spirit.

Refused
by strong blackmen,
she decided
to cast
off
from
Afrikan world-views
for being
senseless
and backward;
replacing it with
a pink mind,
white fenced
enclosed home,
one billion dollars,
no love of
watermelon
or
fried chicken,
and

very determined
to have the
slimy figure
of a
white lass,
though she
be black
as the berry
which
is as
fully ripe
as
a moonless
midnight
in
South Dakota.

IV

Randy

Without knowing who his true foe was, a brother dies over a AT&T and nobody cries. A brother is pushed out of this existence over a phone, and nobody cares; for it is just another nigga gone to thug paradise. Over a phone a brother expires, shoved into the uncaring embrace of death, by one of his own—a sufferer from the caste of amerikkka's untouchable class. He was a thug nigga named Randy, the other's name cannot be used. Randy was around 5'9", 165 pounds, with a tattoo of a star and crescent on his right cheek; dark skin, with a head of hair always worn in french braids. The administration said that it all actually started over a pool ball being thrown out of frustration, out of shame of having lost face: by losing the pool game being played for a few bags of weed. They lie to protect the interest of their partners (AT&T) and the profits procured from the further exploitation of the slave, via the telephone.

Someone was denied their phone time. Words were exchanged—in the tradition of young and old black males. Nasty words, disrespectful words...the situation is defused, but feelings are now involved and each brother plots and plans the demise of the other, clandestinely. The days pass by without incident, but the tension is still thick—for in this hell called prison, the captive is so repressed, so reduced, that the smallest show of disrespect could potentially be carried through to achieve the antithesis of life. The forces of repression allow for such fratricide to occur—fratricide equals genocide when it is caused by an external force, group, bent on pushing out of existence another group; which generally is a weaker and oppressed group. Simply because the system would rather have the slave killing another slave, so as to keep their eyes turned on each other rather than the true source of the suffering.

Over a telephone a brother is killed...AT&T owned, state controlled, profits shared, nigga dead...With his back turned, head bowed, telephone cradled between shoulder and ear, Randy sits—not knowing that the death angel sat in his lap. But all those who have seen death come, seen death inflicted, seen death carried out, felt its presence, and knew that someone was about to be toe-tagged. But Randy did not, for some unknown reason, take note of the tension in his environment, the presence of extreme danger, the forewarning sense of coming combat—the quickening of the pulse, the flaring of the nostrils. His fellow sufferer, his foe, had out-maneuvered him in this sad, but all too common drama plaguing our reality, our long night in the belly of a sick and dying beast. The reality of Blood against Blood!

Randy's foe, without remorse, moved in on him under the cover of a false peace, under the cover of Randy's unawareness of his own coming death. With a jailhouse-constructed knife in hand, a knife which was made from a piece of discarded metal from the concentration camp's auto shop (sharpened on the floor of the dorm's bathroom floor) the death angel moved in for the kill, to get a name, to gain jailhouse fame. All it took was one thrust of his up-raised fist, full of deadly cold steel, and it was all over with—the end of another so young.

A young thug was murdered in another of amerikkka's Prison Industrial Concentration Camps, with a correctional officer nowhere to oversee, to protect, to save the life of this sufferer. No correctional officer made it to the scene of the murder until long after Randy was dead and gone. With what looked so much akin to a drive by, homicide, scene in the war-torn ghettos of amerikkka's internal colonies, on a prison floor, with his mother still on the other end of the phone screaming and crying for her son that was no more, a son that could not hear or care that his foe had done him in; for he had finally got his chance to go see if Tupac was in heaven, a heaven especially made for the sufferer, the ghetto dweller, the thug nigga, the young black male.

In a pool of his own blood, Randy slept the sleepless sleep of the dead. Through a prison-issued sheet he exhaled his very last breath. Without having ever even come close to realizing his human potential, this child of poverty, hardship, and despair expired without any of those who stood around him really caring that one day he had hoped to be able to buy his momma a home down in North Carolina. The prison administration, the keepers and destroyers of the sufferer, had no worry of any public outcry; for, after all, the inmate (#123-456) had died as he lived: without a chance at ever being able to say "I understand now who my true foe is!"

V

He
looked heavenward
this evening,
and
before his eyes
glowed the image
of her beaming
smile
and caressing laugh!

Her
beaming
brown eyes
took hold of his own,
and
led him on
a journey
to a place
far beyond
the furthest
reaches of the stars,
a trillion light years
away from
the evil that
sought to prevent
such a connection,
such a joining.

Off
to the world
where they
had not the need

to live as the
savages lived
at the turn
of this
new century!

Probing
and
touching
the living
essence of
all living things,
they walked
the unseen road
of all tomorrows
to come
and
all yesterdays
gone to no more,
seeing in it
all the
beauty of life
that was to be
found in folk such
as themselves—
human beings
who dared trust,
love,
and
struggle
for a life
in communion with others.

Not

A DISJOINTED SEARCH FOR THE WILL TO LIVE

daring to give
in to that which
is a damn lie,
a sorry attempt
to bring them
back to the evil
that consumes
the mass of humanity;
refusing to say,
"We give up!"

A
trillion stars
away from this moment,
they sit
and
wait for the
changing of
the guard,
moving only
when it is time
for them to
return home.

Without
knowing
how or when,
he finds
himself behind
a word processor,
with her name
on his tongue,
her brown eyes in
his own,

while
writing a piece,
whispering in his heart,
"Thanks so much for the kiss!"...
and
a trillion light years
away,
the changing
of the guard
takes place
once again.
EXUDE, OUT,
closing,
THE END!
In
space,
out there
doing nothing,
lost,
looking for
a reason to live,
a will to live.

Finding
none,
he roams
aimlessly
in a world
ordered
in a manner
that tells him
of his doom
to have
no true reason

A DISJOINTED SEARCH FOR THE WILL TO LIVE

to live other
than
the reason
dictated
by the enemies
of his kind.

In
amerikkka,
in a cage,
in prison,
he sits
and
waits
for his time to come—
his time to be
released to a
freedom
that was never his,
but has
to be made such
by he
and
those of like mind—
warriors in
the
disjointed
search for
the will to live.

AFTERWORD | MARC SALOTTE

I have known Shaka N'Zinga for about seven years now. I first became familiar with him when a friend suggested a few of his poems for inclusion in the newsletter *Claustrophobia* I was helping to edit. Shaka was just beginning to find his voice as a writer at the time, and I read the two poems he submitted not with any particular awe at their style, which was still somewhat awkward, but with a lasting impression at the simplicity and power of his vision and emotion. "The beauty of life is everywhere being destroyed by the INHUMANITY OF MAN" was the type of line that stuck with me. I wondered how someone who had lived through all the subtle nuances of degradation and oppression could allow himself to dare to think in terms of such simple truths. In a situation of unimaginable bureaucratic complexity and inhuman hopelessness, I saw Shaka as that rare person who had set himself the mission of prophesying a beautifully simple and impossible hope for humanity. I printed his two poems, alongside a picture of John Brown to symbolize my own commitment to the same kind of impossible hope Shaka spoke of. We began a correspondence which has lasted to this day.

In everyday life in America, we go through our lives in a kind of alienated daydream. It's not that often that any two people will ever connect—especially if they come from radically different backgrounds. Most of the time, people bring all kinds of hang-ups with them into any kind of interaction they get into. Sometimes, though, a shared point of view can be enough to bring two people out of completely different realities into communication with one another. It can be that simple.

When I first began writing and talking with Shaka, it was one of these things. He called himself an anarchist, and so did I. He had come into consciousness of anarchism in prison, reading and studying all kinds of histories and philosophies trying to find something that would explain why his life was playing itself out in the twisted way it was. He had gone through Islam and more mainstream nationalist worldviews before he started checking into anti-authoritarian ideas. Out here on the street where I was living, dissatisfaction and oppression just kind of simmers in your life, occasionally threatening to boil over; not like in prison where it pours out all over you, scalding you, constantly. It had been a slow path to consciousness for me, not the urgent search it was for Shaka. My path to where I am today shared a lot of the same desperation, rebellion, and points of breakthrough as Shaka's, though of course it was also different in many ways. So here we are, speaking as two comrades—a so-called "white" man who'd never been locked up for any serious time, and a New Afrikan man who came of age in prison. Comrades in the here and now; its amazing how much it means that we look at the world in the same way.

Shaka was arrested in 1989 for the gang-rape and murder—which he did not commit—of a girl at her home near Patterson Park. As a young thug spending his days getting high, looking for a way to make one day flow into the next, he was hanging out with whoever he might run into from day to day, looking for an escape from the constant judgements of society (while at the same time hoping to be alive the next day). On the day of the incident in question he was over at this 21 year-old's house he had met a couple days earlier around the neighborhood. The man turned out to be a wanna-be pimp with a history of rape, but then that's not the first thing you learn about someone you just met. He had drugs and he was willing to get people high, so Shaka and two others, one nineteen years old and the other thirteen, were hanging out for the day. Sometime during the course of the afternoon, high on Rush, this man came up with the idea of raping his wife's daughter, who lived downstairs from him in the basement. Shaka and Jeff, the younger boy, weren't really sure if he was serious, but didn't want to stay around and find out. They walked down the block to the corner store, and when they returned and looked in the window, Jean Rae Wantland had been suffocated to death.

Three months later, the body was found and within a week, Shaka and two others were arrested in connection. Although Jeff's first statement to the police cleared Shaka, he was arrested nonetheless; arrested as a fifteen-year-old New Afrikan man-child on the streets of Baltimore, as a boy who the system had given up on, or rather, never even really intended to give a fair chance to. He was arrested as a "problem child," who had always had trouble conforming to the disciplines of a school system that dulls your mind and senses, a broken family system that constantly stresses your emotions, and a life of poverty where day to day survival is up in the air. And just as much as any of these other reasons, he was arrested as a New Afrikan youth in a crime where the victim was white, and the two perpetrators were grown white men (one of whom was even the victim's stepfather) who "couldn't have done such a thing on their own." Shaka was a perfect scapegoat.

Now the first thing that white "justice" does to its victims is to strip them of any responsibility, any accountability—in the sense of power to be able to define, to explain the circumstances, to accept or refuse blame—for their own actual actions. Instead of being directly confronted by the consequences of the conflict you were involved in, you "get your day in court"—a chance to follow the state's script and give it legitimacy in its control over all of us. And at the end of the day, you're not a "criminal" cause of what you do, you're a criminal cause of who you are, and where you happen to be. And we internalize this to the point where we forget the distinction. That's what I'm trying to get at here. Society as a whole (if it can be said that there exists such a thing) needs to look at how it deals with anti-social behavior and the people it assumes are committing it. People whose loved ones and friends have gotten caught up in the court/prison system need to learn to see them for who they are, human beings in essence and mind whose bodies have gotten trapped in a negative and self-perpetuating cycle they had no part in creating. And those of us who are supporting prisoners need to examine our preconceptions and stereotypes of "innocence" and "guilt," even when we think we've gotten over the system's voice repeating in our heads.

Since slavery days, the public presentation of New Afrikan men has always been based in a large part on a carefully crafted fear of New Afrikan male sexuality, whether as "rapists" who needed strict policing and punishment or as "tempters" who needed to be strictly segregated so as not to corrupt white women and men. This dialectic has been seething beneath the surface all this time, and its impossible to even talk about the insane numbers of New Afrikan men in prison without wondering how many of them were victims of this very stereotype before they were declared "guilty" by a white legal system that as a whole is guilty of rape and murder on a scale out of all proportion to the worst man in prison. The myth of the Black rapist has been one tool by which "white power" - whether the State or the Klan - has been able to terrorize, attack and disable New Afrikan communities with the fervent support of white communities. This is why Shaka was arrested.

Then there is the horrific act itself. The type of twisted mentality where people can have so little respect for each other that an eighteen-year-old woman can be attacked, raped, and murdered, and in such a casual way. Shaka and Jean are in the same boat, really, allies against a way of life that served them both death sentences. Jean Wantland was raped and killed ultimately because of the ideological construction of women's sexuality as submissive and the construction of a male sexuality that rapes 1 in 3 women at some point in their life. Shaka has sat in prison for fourteen years on a 40 year sentence because as a New Afrikan male, "society" insisted his sexuality was predatory and bestial. Just as society and the court was prepared to see Shaka as a rapist and murderer, Jean was to be seen as sexual object, weak and without will. These are the fantasies of generations of white men who have ruled. These fantasies have ruled for generations. They are ideological cover for a strategy of divide and rule.

During Shaka's first few days in jail (feeling sick, having just been beaten up, still barely able to read at all, let alone make sense of the charges against him), he got a visit from a lawyer, a blond-haired blue-eyed con job in a suit and tie. The man never identified himself—to this day Shaka isn't sure whether he was an assistant to the public defender who represented him or to the state's attorney—and the only advice he gave, without even having looked over the case, was to plead guilty. "It doesn't matter whether you did it or not. You're black, the victim was white, and they're not gonna want to hear your side."

This is one further step in the process of enforcing the master/slave consciousness. When the system depends on the public perception of New Afrikan men as a "dangerous class"—and particularly so in relation to white women—it needs to not only constantly reinforce that image in the minds of "white" people, but it needs to continually devote itself to convincing New Afrikans to accept and play along with that image. From that day onward, that was basically how Shaka thought of himself. Although he knew he hadn't taken part in the rape and murder of the young woman, he felt as though the conviction, the brand of being seen as a rapist and killer, was just another unfairness of the system that was out of his control; that he had to accept that. He felt, and actually believed, that he was "just a criminal" because of who he was, that there was no use debating that and claiming his innocence. And in addition, that's how I always felt unconsciously at first while supporting him. To me, his complicity—at least—in the crime he had been convicted of was always a given, something out of anyone's control; something that was a fait accompli in the system, whatever the truth might have been. I saw myself as supporting a Black man who had been driven to crime by a white social system, and who was given an excessive punishment by a criminal justice system that is more interested in keeping New Afrikan people under its control than in solving the social problems that cause "crime." All this is true, but the truth is a lot deeper than any of this.

While in prison, Shaka came into all kinds of new consciousness. In this pamphlet he speaks of how he began to see that he was much more than just a criminal, a thug, a "nigga"—that he was an African, a New Afrikan, and that there was plenty to be proud of in that identity and heritage. In particular, he talks about the role that older "conscious" prisoners—among others, Black Panther veteran Marshall "Eddie" Conway, who has been locked up for over 25 years on a political frame-up — played in helping him come to that understanding. He learned to read and write, studied history, politics, and culture, began to write poetry and fiction, explored a number of philosophies, and started to take on the immense responsibilities of educating and organizing the younger brothers who were getting locked up to see themselves as, and be, human beings with pride and dignity.

In the process of his studies, he began to learn little bits of the oppressor's law, and started to review the legal proceedings that landed him in his dark cell in the first place. Out of documents he was able to obtain from the police and the courts, he found all kinds of blatant inconsistencies in his trial that proved the truth of what the man had told him his first days in the lock-up. It really didn't matter to the cops and the courts whether or not he was guilty, as a matter of procedure he would be run through the system and "found" guilty. The state's "star witness," the thirteen-year-old boy who had been with Shaka and the two grown men who actually committed the crimes in question, under initial questioning gave a statement saying that he and Shaka hadn't wanted to take part, and had even left the house during the assault. The next day, an arrest warrant was put out for Shaka—allegedly on the "evidence" of this youth's testimony. The day after that, under further questioning (and no doubt a good deal of pressure,) this boy changed his story, this time naming Shaka as the main perpetrator, and the one who pushed all the others into committing this crime. In the grand jury transcripts (the hearings were two days later) two and a half pages of text are taken up by threats like these:

> "*if you cooperate and tell us the truth—that is tell us what you told the police in your **second** statement to the police...*"
> "Yes, sir."

AFTERWORD BY MARC SALOTTE

> "However, if we find out that you lied to us... you could, first of all, be charged with a crime called perjury... you could be waived to the adult court and charged and tried as an adult where you could face up to a ten year sentence for perjury. Do you understand that?"
>
> "Yes, sir."
>
> "...you tell us a different story today and... we can not only charge you with perjury, we can charge you with murder. Do you understand that?"
>
> "Yes, sir."

This kind of trial makes it pretty obvious that the state would act exactly like the mysterious lawyer had warned Shaka: there is nothing easier for them than to frame-up and send away a New Afrikan street youth and petty hustler. Not only is it easy, the state makes a policy of it. What do you think "zero tolerance" is? Shaka wasn't framed out of any particular beef the court had with him, but as a matter of policy for troublesome working class youth who needed to be dealt with, as a class. Read this book with this in mind, but at the same time, read it with an understanding that Shaka is so much more than his involvement in a situation that now defines his life as a "convict."

Never let yourself become so deadened by the madness of society that you can say that "its nothing" that a woman is brutally raped and killed or that any kind of anti-human crime is perpetrated in our communities. But at the same time, never let yourself be fooled by the search for scapegoats the system promotes to cover up its own failings. In the puppet show, where one fragment of humanity is set against another in an endless series of feuds, we are all cut and degraded while the puppet master looks on and laughs.

Help us in assisting Shaka as he attempts to prove his legal innocence in a crime which he did not participate in, but was implicated in by circumstances of a whirlwind so much bigger than him, or any one of us. But just as importantly, read his words as those of a comrade, a writer, a revolutionary who is struggling to rise above the conditions life has forced on him, and point others in a direction to do the same.

A WORD FROM AN ELDER | IDRIS ALAOMA

The well known and respected principle that "men are equal" can best be illustrated in their conscious endeavors. In this instance it is the equality of the Black intellectual and revolutionary writers of today. It was during the latter months of 1994, in the Writer's Club Inc., when I first met Shaka N'Zinga. From our first encounters and through my observations of him, in the books and periodicals he read, and in my reading of his writings at that time, I suspected Shaka held the potential to not only be an equal with any of today's Black intellectuals and revolutionary writers.

In fact it was immediately clear that Shaka had already decided he was aspiring to not just be an equal, but to far exceed many of them and claim for himself a place as one of today's New Afrikan Revolutionary writers.

Of course he has set himself an arduous task; however, I am confident he will succeed for he is a New Afrikan warrior. His pen is his spear and his wisdom, knowledge, and understanding of the intellectual and revolutionary writers of today is his shield.

The intellectual writer writes with regards to the old universal abstract that Black people and White people may live together in peace in the new world. Shaka, as I have said, is a New Afrikan revolutionary writer, who has long perceived that most whites have lost interest in remaining or co-existing.

I think Shaka N'Zinga's success as a writer will be his subtle combinations of what is best of these two equals into the understanding and expression of who is Shaka N'Zinga.

SHAKA N'ZINGA (2002)